Undeniable Risk

R.I.S.C. Series Book 9
Anna Blakely

Savage Risk
R.I.S.C. Series 9
First Edition
Copyright © 2021 Anna Blakely
All rights reserved.
All cover art and logo Copyright © 2021
Publisher: Aces Press
Cover by Lori Jackson Design
Proofreading by Angie Springs, Christine Hall and Kim Ruiz

All rights reserved. No part of this book may be reproduced in any form or by any electronic or mechanical means, including information storage and retrieval systems—except in the case of brief quotations embodied in critical articles or reviews—without permission in writing from the author.

This book is a work of fiction. The names, characters, and places portrayed in this book are entirely products of the author's imagination or used fictitiously. Any resemblance to actual events, locales, or persons, living or dead, is entirely coincidental and not intended by the author.

The unauthorized reproduction or distribution of this copyrighted work is illegal. Criminal copyright infringement, including infringement without monetary gain, is investigated by the FBI and is punishable by up to five years in federal prison and a fine of $250,000.00.

If you find any eBooks being sold or shared illegally, please contact the author at anna@annablakelycom.

Dedication

For my readers. Your continued love and support for my stories and characters are why I do what I do.
XOXO ~
Anna

About the Book

A man dedicated to fighting injustice. A woman devoted to saving lives. A ruthless leader determined to see them both dead.

Homeland Agent Jason Ryker lives for his job, often blurring the lines between right and wrong for the greater good. But when the only woman ever to steal his focus—and his heart—becomes the target of a ruthless killer, there are no more lines. There's only her.

Dr. Sophia Ruiz has the career she's always dreamed of, but her personal life is a nightmare. Tall, dark, and stoically handsome Jason Ryker pushes all her female buttons. But there's a problem: he barely knows she exists. So when Sophie finds herself in danger, she's shocked to see the aloof Homeland Agent risking his life to keep her safe.

As sparks between them fly, Sophie is thrown headfirst into another nightmare. One with deadly consequences. With time running out, it's up to Jason and the members of R.I.S.C. to save Sophie from the madman—before it's too late.

Prologue

Four years ago...

"She's here."

Looking away from the file on his desk, Jason Ryker gave his assistant a nod. "Bring her in."

"This one's nice." Betty smiled. "Really nice. And pretty. I think she's a keeper."

"This is a job interview, Betty. Not a blind date."

With a chuckle, the older woman's kind smile grew even wider. "I know it's an interview, and I've seen her resume. Very impressive. All I'm saying is this new hospital of yours will be serving a select group of patients. Bedside manner is going to be just as important as the pedigree hanging on those shiny new walls."

Jason supposed the woman had a point. *She usually does.*

The men and women they'd serve would expect compassion as well as competence. He made a mental note to keep that in mind moving forward.

He'd already given the green light on a handful of applicants, but construction on Homeland's private medical center—a product of his own creation—would be complete in a few short months. If they wanted to open their doors on time, he needed to push through the rest of the interviews quickly.

Some days he still found himself surprised that the powers that be had backed his idea for the new hospital. Thankfully, they saw the need for it as much as he did.

Being in charge of his own covert black ops unit, Jason had dealt with his fair share of injured operatives. Despite the time and planning that went into every mission he spearheaded, unexpected things happened, and his people sometimes got hurt.

When they did, they needed a place where they could go without fear of the staff and local authorities getting too involved.

Bullet wounds, injuries from explosives, stab wounds...those types of injuries brought on a lot of damn questions. Questions that—due to the classified nature of their jobs—his people were not allowed to answer.

Jason first got the idea for the private hospital after one of the teams under him got caught up in a particularly harry op on U.S. soil. Several of his men were injured, and it was a pain in the ass when the emergency room staff called in local authorities.

Right then, Jason knew what Homeland needed to do.

After jumping through the hoops covered in red tape, his plan was approved, and they now had a secure facility where government officials, area military personnel, and alphabet agency employees could go to be treated by some of the best doctors in the country.

All without having to worry about reporters catching wind of it and making their health concerns the headlines for the six o'clock news.

It wouldn't be open to the general public. There were plenty of excellent hospitals in Dallas where they could go for medical care.

No, this facility had been built with a heightened level of security to the point the President of the United States could be treated there, and the outside world would never know it.

"Agent Ryker." Betty tore through his thoughts. "This is Dr. Sophia Ruiz. Dr. Ruiz, this is Agent Jason Ryker, the man responsible for building the hospital where you'll be working."

"Betty." He said her name as a warning.

He stood and walked around his desk, his narrowed gaze zeroing in on the meddling woman. Betty was looking back at him with a knowing smirk, making him want to growl at her slip of the tongue that wasn't a slip at all.

I swear, if the woman wasn't such an invaluable asset...

"Thank you, Betty." He gave her a tight smile. "Please close the door behind you."

Waiting for the daring woman to leave, Jason's focus shifted to the applicant waiting to be interviewed. The air in his lugs froze, and it was only by the grace of God and a shit ton of training that he was able to school his expression and not give away his unexpected reaction.

Betty was wrong when she'd called this woman pretty. She was far, far more than that.

She's stunning.

As he continued walking toward her, Jason quickly assessed her appearance without making it obvious. The last thing he needed was a sexual harassment lawsuit hanging over his damn head.

Standing well below his six-two frame, she had a body made for sin with curves in all the right places. His dick twitched behind his pants, and he was thankful as fuck for the jacket covering his swelling zipper.

Even through the ultra-professional blouse and suit jacket, Jason could make out the swells of two perfectly proportioned breasts. From beneath her skirt's acceptable hemline, he noticed her legs were tan and toned. A runner, if he had to guess.

Her dark hair was pulled back in a way that her waves rested atop the crown of her head. A few wavy strands framed her face in a way that made him want to tuck them behind her adorable ears, and her face...

Lord have mercy, she had the most beautiful face he'd ever seen.

Olive skin that looked smooth and flawless. Big, round, intelligent eyes the color of milk chocolate, and a full, perfectly bow-shaped mouth that had him longing for a taste.

But it was the set of twin dimples—one on each of her soft, kissable cheeks—that intrigued Jason the most.

"Nice to meet you, Agent Ryker." She held out a hand and smiled.

Damn, those dimples just got deeper.

Keeping himself in check, Jason took hold of her delicate hand and squeezed. The strength in her grasp surprised him, though it probably shouldn't.

Something in her pretty eyes told him this woman was a force to be reckoned with.

"Dr. Ruiz."

"Please, call me Sophie."

"Sophie." He gave her a slight nod.

Though he hated to, Jason released her hand and gestured toward one of the two leather chairs facing his desk. "Please, have a seat."

"Thank you. Oh, and here." She handed him a slim, black portfolio. "My CV is in there, as well as several professional references."

A CV, or curriculum vitae, was a clinical medical professional's version of a resume.

With the portfolio in hand, Jason made his way back to his chair and sat down at his desk.

During the course of the next hour, he proceeded to ask the standard interview questions, being sure not to delve into anything that could be considered personal.

Which was hard as hell, because he found himself wanting to know anything and everything about the intriguing woman.

Just two questions in, he'd already made the decision to hire her. Not because she was the most beautiful woman he'd ever seen. In fact, that made things even harder.

Pun intended.

Since the hospital was his baby, he'd most likely be spending a few days a week there. At least in the beginning. Once it was up and running, he'd still need to meet regularly with the facility director.

Which meant he was going to be seeing a lot of Dr. Ruiz.

Wish I could see all of her.

The sudden and highly inappropriate thought had Jason damn near shooting out of his chair.

This woman was going to be working for him. Well, not directly. Technically, her boss would be the hospital's Chief Medical Officer.

He shouldn't be thinking of a future Homeland employee in such a manner. He was a professional, for Christ's sake. And so was she.

"Thank you for your time, Dr. Ruiz." Jason stood and went back around to her. "There are still a few final steps before I can officially offer you the job, but I'll be contacting HR to let them know they can begin the hiring process."

"Really?" Those big eyes lit up as she held out her hand for the second time. "Thank you so much, Agent Ryker. You won't regret this."

He wasn't so sure about that.

"Jason." He took her hand in his, using the innocent opportunity to touch her once again. "You can call me Jason."

You can call me Jason? Seriously? Why not just go ahead and tell her you want to strip her down and drive yourself balls deep into her delectable body?

Giving himself a mental smack, he somehow managed to keep his demeanor professional. Thankfully, if the gorgeous doctor suspected his wildly inappropriate thoughts, she didn't let on.

With a final goodbye, Jason stood at his doorway, watching the impressive woman walk away. Feeling as though he'd just made the biggest mistake of his life, he went to Betty's office and instructed her to get the paperwork rolling.

"Told you," she said with a smartass grin.

Responding with nothing more than a low grunt, he returned to his office and shut the door. Once inside, he drew in his first real breath since meeting Sophie.

His reaction to her was ridiculous. He'd known attractive women before. Even slept with them, on occasion. So why the hell he felt like his world had just turned on its axis was beyond his comprehension.

She's a gorgeous, professional woman, and Homeland is lucky to have her.

The voice in his head was right. Jason knew his decision to hire Dr. Ruiz was based solely on her credentials and experience, and nothing more. He'd just have to make damn sure he stayed as far away from her as he could.

Otherwise, he was bound to do something stupid like pull her in his arms and kiss her.

Chapter 1

Present Day Djibouti, Africa...

Another explosion lit the early morning sky. Dr. Sophia Ruiz couldn't tell where it had originated from, but she did know it was far too close for comfort.

From her place near the window, she looked back at her patient. Relieved the man's medically induced coma kept him unaware of the violence surrounding them.

"I can't believe this is happening." Christine, one of the nurses who'd traveled to Djibouti with the same volunteer group as Sophie stood in the corner farthest from the window.

In her forties, the Wisconsin native was sweet but tough. Of course, even the strongest person would be scared under these circumstances.

Hell, I'm terrified.

"I know." Sophie crossed her arms in front of her and nodded. "But we'll be okay. The hospital chief came in while you were in the restroom. He said someone from Camp Lemonnier called. They're sending a Naval unit to come get us."

Camp Lemonnier was a United States Naval Expeditionary Base located near the Djibouti-Ambouli International Airport. It was the only permanent U.S. military base in Africa.

Lucky for them, it wasn't too far from the hospital they were in, now. Sophie just prayed the team they were sending got here sooner, rather than later.

Since coming here three weeks ago, she'd witnessed her fair share of aggressive behavior by some in the area. But nothing more than what she'd been warned about by the AMOVA representative when she'd initially agreed to the trip.

AMOVA—which stood for American Medical Organization for Volunteer Aid—was a non-profit organization that traveled all over the world to help those in need. The doctors and nurses who joined would take temporary assignments in countries with great deficiencies in supplies and properly trained medical professionals.

Sophie and her temporary colleagues had not only been helping treat patients in the poverty-stricken city of Djibouti and its surrounding area, but they'd also spent time training the doctors and nurses at one of the local hospitals in the city.

In addition to that, two days a week they'd been traveling to Chabelley—a small village located about seven miles southwest of Djibouti. There, they set up a makeshift clinic for those unable to travel into the city.

By and large, the interactions Sophie and the others had experienced were positive. Most locals were grateful for the added medical aid, and expressed their thanks with smiles, handshakes, and hugs.

Of course, like most areas such as this, there were also radical groups present. Terrorists who'd love nothing more than to kidnap American aid workers, either for profit or as a voice to push their horrific agendas.

Until now, the worst Sophie had personally witnessed were a few minor physical assaults on the streets. Not that those were okay, by any means. But they were nothing compared to what had been happening during the last twenty or so hours.

Bombs detonating in the distance. Car alarms blaring and emergency sirens screaming. Loud, sporadic pops of gunfire.

It was everything she'd seen on TV and in the movies but never dreamed she'd have to experience in real life. She couldn't imagine living in a place where this sort of violence was considered the norm.

Sophie also couldn't imagine what it was like for the heroic military men and women who ran headfirst into the line of fire.

The minute they signed their names on that dotted line, they agreed to risk their lives for people they'd never met before. Innocent strangers needing protection from the terroristic wrath some men felt they had the right to bestow upon the world.

As if reading her most recent thoughts, Christine sat down in the chair next to the patient's bed and sighed.

"Part of me hates knowing American soldiers are out there right now, risking their lives just to get to us. But at the same time, I'm really freaking glad they are." Trepidation oozed from the woman's big, brown eyes as she looked up at her. "Does that make me a horrible person?"

"No." Sophie shook her head. "It makes you human."

At least, that's what she'd been telling herself to justify the *hurry up and get here* thoughts that had been spinning through her *own* mind.

Sophie had always considered herself to be a pretty tough cookie. As an emergency room doctor, she had to be. But she wasn't trained in combat, and she sure as heck didn't have a death wish.

As much as she hated the idea of leaving the local medical staff and their patients behind, Sophie knew she'd be of no use to anyone if she got herself killed trying to be a martyr.

Still, as the volunteer doctor in charge of today's shift, it was up to her to remain calm. For her staff and their patients.

Another round of successive gunfire filled the night air, making her muscles tense. Moving the curtain to the side, Sophie peeked past the thick material to see if there was any immediate danger near their building.

"Dr. Sophia Ruiz?"

Hearing her name, Sophie spun her head around with a start.

A man stood in the doorway, black paint smeared from below his eyes to just above his dark beard.

Carrying what appeared to be an M4 assault rifle, the newcomer was dressed in head-to-toe desert camo. Complete with a combat helmet, coms, and night vision goggles that had been pushed up and out of the way.

But it was the American Flag patch on the center of the man's chest that sent relief flowing through Sophie's system.

He's American.

"Oh, thank God!" Christine shot up out of the chair.

Without looking at the other woman, the man kept his eyes locked with Sophie's. "Are you Dr.—"

"Sophia Ruiz," she finished for him. "Yes, that's me."

"Ma'am, I'm Master Chief Scott Warren with the United States Navy SEALS. I'm here to get you to safety."

So not a soldier. An operator.

Working her every-day job at Homeland Security's private medical facility back home in Dallas, Sophie had treated enough military patients to know the different titles each branch preferred to be called. One thing she'd quickly learned was that SEALS were *never* to be called soldier.

More than anything, Sophie wanted to follow this operator out that door and never look back. She wanted to be away from the danger and violence raining down on the city of Djibouti. To be home in the warmth and comfort of her own bed.

Did that make her weak or lessen her dedication to taking care of those in need? She didn't think so. At least, she prayed it didn't.

Like she'd told Christine...she was human. Yes, she'd come here to help the less fortunate, and for the past three weeks, she had. Intentionally keeping herself in harm's way with no backup or professional training wouldn't make her brave. It would make her foolish.

Even so, the doctor in her couldn't help but ask the SEAL, "What about the patients?"

She glanced toward the man lying in the bed next to her, oblivious of the situation surrounding him. The Master Chief's gaze followed hers.

"They'll be taken care of."

Sophie swallowed. "How can you be sure?"

"There's another team on their way here to keep guard over the patients who were unable to be transported when the riots began."

That was good news. *Really* good. There was just one more thing.

"What about the rest of the volunteers?"

There were eight of them in all, including a well-known journalist who'd joined the trip last minute to do a story on the work they were doing in the war-torn city.

"My team has been assigned to locate you and your group, and escort you out of harm's way. The other men are rounding up the remaining volunteers on the list as we speak. So far, the building remains clear of insurgents, but if things keep progressing the way they have been, that won't last forever. We need to go. Now."

Master Chief Warren's voice was calm and steady, but it was clear he was anxious to get the heck out of Dodge.

"You don't have to tell me twice." Christina grabbed her bag from its place on the floor and walked to the door.

They'd both gotten their things from the lockers in the staff lounge earlier, before coming to this room to wait for reinforcements.

Knowing there really wasn't anything more she could do, Sophie gave her patient a parting glance before removing the white coat the hospital had provided and laying it across the foot of the bed.

Walking over to the cheap, particle board armoire on the other side of the room, she grabbed the messenger bag she used as a purse-slash-emergency medical bag and followed Master Chief Warren and Christine out into the hallway.

Bypassing the elevators, the three entered the nearest stairwell and began their descent. They'd started on the fourth floor, but it didn't take long before they were approaching the first floor.

"These things always give me the creeps," Christine muttered as they took the steps as quickly and carefully as possible. "Makes me think of the clichéd movies where the girl gets attacked by a masked man while in the stairwell alone."

Behind her, Sophia chuckled. "Well, seeing as how we're following a sort-of masked man of our own, I'd say our chances of survival are pretty good."

The words had no more passed her lips when the door at the bottom of the stairs flew open and bullets began to fly.

Master Chief Warren returned fire, shouting over his shoulder for the two women to get down. When the enemy gunfire temporarily ceased, he motioned for them to run back up the stairs and then used his comms to call for his team.

Shooting another round of bullets at the open doorway, he did his best to keep his voice low as he ordered Sophie and Christine to find the nearest room and hide.

Following the man's orders, Sophie grabbed hold of Christine's hand and pulled her back up the stairs and through the first door they came to. After checking both ways to make sure the coast was clear, she then led the other woman into the first patient room she saw.

Blowing out a breath, she was glad as hell to find it unoccupied. The last thing she wanted was to lead whoever was shooting at them into a helpless patient's room.

"Ohmygod!" Christine blurted. "I can't believe we just got shot at!"

"Shh!" Sophie reminded her to keep quiet. Looking around the room, she found the only hiding place available...the other side of the bed. "Come on!"

Running around the foot of the bed, they crouched down between it and a small, metal shelf half-filled with various medical supplies.

"What are we going to do?" Christine looked to her with wide, frightened eyes.

Sophie whispered as softly as she could. "We're going to wait for Master Chief Warren to come get us."

"What if he doesn't? Sophie, he's out there all by himself."

"I heard him calling for his team before we ran back up the stairs. They're SEALS. They'll find him."

She just prayed they got to him in time.

"This is unreal." Christine shook her head. "This was supposed to be a safe volunteer mission. Shit like this wasn't supposed to happen to us."

"This shouldn't happen to anyone," Sophie commented quietly.

"Good point."

She held up a hand. "I think someone's coming."

With her heart racing and the sound of blood rushing past her ears, Sophie reached for Christine's hand and held on tight.

Booted footfalls sounded from the hallway. Their beat strong and steady as their owners marched closer to the room. Alarm crossed over Christine's face, but she remained silent.

They both did.

The footfalls stopped. Sophie held her breath and waited. Terror thundered down on her as the agonizing seconds passed by. Just when she thought whoever was out there had gone, the door flung open, and a group of angry men stormed the room.

Oh, god!

Without a word, one of the men rounded the bed and pointed his gun at Sophie's head.

She'd always believed a person's life was supposed to flash before their eyes. That's what everyone said, right? That's what she'd seen on TV and in the movies.

When a person was faced with imminent death, their minds were supposed to become filled with wonderful, cherished memories. Memories of beloved family members and friends. Important milestones they'd achieved during their time here on Earth.

Flashes of first loves and the one who got away.

Those were the things Sophie *expected* to see. Instead, the group of men with very large guns and cold, evil eyes was all that filled her vision.

That and the barrel of his long, black rifle.

"My name is Dr. Sophia Ruiz," she blurted, her voice surprisingly steady. "I'm part of a volunteer group serving the people of Djibouti and the nearby villages."

She thought about Master Chief. Had he survived? Given her current situation, Sophie knew his chances weren't good.

She shot Christine a quick glance from over her shoulder. The other woman was currently frozen with the same terror that had turned Sophie's blood to ice.

Christine was right. This wasn't supposed to happen.

Before today, their trip had been a pleasant experience. It was true, the city of Djibouti was inundated with unimaginable poverty. But despite the poor conditions and the active terrorist presence, the locals in both communities had been warm and hospitable to Sophie and the other members of her volunteer group.

These men, however—the ones staring back at them with their big guns and snarling grins—were anything but warm.

"My name is Dr. Sophia Ruiz," she repeated. Only this time, she spoke the words in Arabic. "I'm part of a volunteer group serving the people of Djibouti and the nearby villages."

"Shut up!" the man pointing his gun at her growled. Though his accent was heavy, his English was easily understood.

Taking a step closer, he kept his weapon steady. His narrowed eyes remained trained on hers.

Behind her, Christine whimpered slightly, so Sophie gave her new friend's hand a gentle squeeze and forced herself to try again.

"I'm the doctor in charge, here. What is it you want from us?"

"Right now, I want you to remember your place."

Her place?

Oh, right. Because I'm a woman.

With her back teeth ground together, Sophie drew in a breath and relaxed her jaw. "Do you or your men need medical attention?" She already knew the answer. None were visibly injured in any way. "We can help with whatever it is you nee—"

Pain exploded across Sophie's cheek as the asshole backhanded her. The small shelf to her left toppled over as she tried to grab onto its metal frame.

"Sophie!" Christine cried out her name.

Though she tried to avoid it, Sophie lost her grip on Christine's hand. She landed with a thud on the cold, tiled floor next to the fallen shelf and scattered supplies.

"*I* am the one in charge here," the jerk who'd struck her hissed angrily. "Not you."

"Was that really necessary, Abdul?" one of the other two men asked.

"You want to join her on the ground?"

While the two men continued bickering back and forth, Sophie breathed through the throbbing pain and pushed herself back up to her feet.

A tear slid free, falling down over her tender cheek. Not because she was crying, but because the forceful blow had caused her eye to water.

She held a hand to the side of her face, the skin there stinging and hot to the touch. *Damn, that hurt.*

"I-I meant no disrespect," she told the man softly.

"You speaking to me without permission is disrespect."

Though it may very well earn her another bruise, Sophie said, "Just tell me what it is you want."

"The journalist. Where is he?"

Wait. What?

Sophie frowned. Why would these men be after Colton?

"Tell me where he is, and you and your friend will live."

Something about the way he said it—something in his angry, dark eyes—told Sophie he was lying. He had no intentions of letting her or the others go.

I'm not ready to die.

She also didn't want to see these men hurt Colton. They were clearly after him for a reason, and whatever that was, it couldn't be good.

This part of the world was notorious for kidnapping and torturing journalists. Especially ones like Colton Moore, who'd written several investigative stories exposing the various Middle East terrorist groups.

While Sophie didn't know him very well, Colton had been friendly and pleasant to be around during the short time they'd all spent together.

"He's not here," she told the man.

Colton had been with her when the Chief informed them the Navy was sending a team to escort them out of the building. He'd gone with her and Christine to the staff area to get their things, but instead of following them to the room where they'd been waiting previously, he'd said he had something he had to take care of, first.

Before Sophie could stop him, he left. She hadn't seen him since.

"You lie," the man with the gun took a step closer.

"I'm not." She shook her head. "H-he wasn't feeling well, so he took the rest of the day off."

Okay, that last part was a lie. But if they were specifically looking for Colton and thought he wasn't in the building, maybe they would let her and Christine go.

Please let him believe me. Please, please believe me.

The man in charge looked around the room. In one, quick glance, he could see there was nowhere Colton could be hiding. To one of the others who'd come with him, he ordered, "Check the other rooms in this hallway."

Doing as instructed, the two men left in search of their target. Sophie's mind raced to figure out what she would do if Colton returned before these jerks left. In reality, she knew there was nothing she *could* do.

Fighting them would be futile. They were big and strong, armed to the teeth, and most likely trained in hand-to-hand combat.

She and Christine were none of those things.

Several long, agonizing minutes passed before the others returned. "He's not here. Not on this floor, at least."

Inside, Sophie was breathing a huge sigh of relief. Outwardly, she schooled her expression so they wouldn't have any reason to doubt what she'd told them.

If they asked which hotel they were staying at, she'd lie. Then she'd figure out a way to warn Colton he was in danger.

Because these weren't the type of men to give up easily.

The one in charge, the one still pointing his gun at her, thought for a moment before biting out a sharp, "Call him."

Sophie's stomach dropped. "What?"

"Call Mr. Moore. Tell him you need him to come here."

"No." The refusal was out before she could stop it.

Anger reddened the man's face as he stormed toward her. "How dare you defy me!"

Fear nearly choked her to the point she had to physically work to keep her body from trembling. She had no interest in being a martyr, but she also couldn't bring herself to do what this man was asking.

"I'm not going to lure an innocent man here simply so you can…do whatever it is you plan to do to him."

Her decision may have just cost Sophie her life ,but she also couldn't knowingly put Colton—or any other person—in danger.

The man stood directly in front of her, now. His hot, rancid breath hit her face as he spoke, nearly making her gag. "Call. Him."

With her heart in her throat, she kept her spine straight and shook her head.

"No."

He pressed the tip of his gun against her forehead, the cold metal cutting into the delicate skin there. "If you do not call your journalist friend, I will send a bullet straight through your brain."

Something did flash through her mind, just then. It wasn't a childhood memory, or even anything of the sort. It was a man's face.

A man she thought about often but barely knew.

Well, isn't that great. I'm about to die, and out of everything I could think of, the one and only regret I have is the last thing playing through my mind?

"Sophie."

Christine's pleading voice pulled her away from the crazy thought.

From her tone, it was clear the other woman wanted her to make the call. Not that Sophie could blame her. They were both seconds away from being murdered, and the only possible way out was to do what the man said.

It was an impossible position to be in. Call Colton and lure him into a deadly trap or refuse and die.

"I don't have his number," she spoke her second lie.

Why the hell hadn't she thought to say that, sooner?

The man lowered his weapon, and both she and Christine breathed a sigh of relief. Their respite was short-lived, however, because in the very next second, the man's free hand was squeezing her neck so tightly, she was gasping for air.

"You said you were the doctor in charge. That means you have all of the volunteers' numbers saved in the phone provided by AMOVA."

What the...how did this man know that?

He must've seen the realization cross over her because he smiled, then. "That's right. I would love nothing more than to teach that lying, deceitful mouth of yours a lesson. Unfortunately, I do not have the time. So, I will simply kill you and she will make the call, instead."

He shoved her to the side, her ribs landing hard against the bed's metal railing. Sucking in a breath, Sophie ignored the pain and grabbed hold of the cold steel to keep from falling again.

When she spun her head around, she saw the man's gun rising toward her once more. This time, however, she knew no amount of talking would save her.

"Please!" Christine begged him to stop. "Don't!"

A deafening bang filled the room. Sophie squeezed her eyes shut and waited for the bullet to strike.

It never did.

There were two more shots fired, and then...

"Sophia!"

That voice.

God, was she actually dead, after all? It was the only explanation she could think of as to why she was hearing *his* voice here, in this room.

Moving slowly, Sophie peeled her eyes open, shocked by what she was seeing.

The man who'd threatened to kill her was dead, his lifeless body lying in a crumpled heap at her feet. His two buddies had also been shot. Both having died in the exact spots where they'd been standing.

Another man was there...the same one she saw in her mind during what she believed would be her last seconds alive. Only this was a different Jason Ryker than the one she'd imagined in her dreams.

The Jason she knew wore perfectly pressed suits and his hair was almost never out of place. He was professional to a fault, and never ever showed any signs of real emotion.

At least not during the times she'd been around him.

But this Jason...the one who'd appeared out of nowhere as if she'd somehow conjured him up herself...he wasn't wearing a suit.

With a long gun in one hand, he was dressed in a helmet and black t-shirt that stretched over his muscles in the most magnificent way. His lower half was covered with matching black combat pants and boots, and protecting his broad chest was a bullet resistant vest.

And he was rushing toward her like a man on a mission.

"Jason?" Sophie blinked at the Homeland agent's larger-than-life image, her mind racing to comprehend what had just happened.

Without a word, he pulled her into his arms and held on as if he never wanted to let go.

With an oof, she returned the unexpected gesture, feeling as if she'd been thrown into some other realm. An alternate reality where the man holding her cared about her in ways she'd only dreamed about.

"W-what are you doing here?" The words came out muffled, thanks to her face being pressed against his hard chest.

Ignoring the question, Jason pulled away and began frantically running his hands along her body as if he were assessing her for injuries.

"Did he touch you?" He rasped. "Are you hurt?"

What is happening right now?

"I-I'm fine." She stood stunned, following his hands with her gaze as they moved down the length of her arms. "Jason, what are you—"

"That fucking bastard."

His deep growl had Sophie's head snapping back up. Her breath caught in her throat when she realized his intense, dark chocolate eyes were zeroed in on her right cheek.

The same one that had been hit.

The level of emotion pouring off Jason took her by complete surprise. This was a man who was always in control. *Always.*

But the way he's looking at me now...

"It's nothing." Without even thinking, Sophie placed her hand against his chest to reassure him. "Really, I'm okay."

His heart pounded hard beneath her palm, its frantic beat nearly matching hers exactly.

Angry eyes softened when they slid from her cheek to meet her gaze, and for just a second, she saw something in them that sent her pulse racing.

In that brief, fleeting moment, however, Sophie caught a glimpse of the man behind the curtain. The *real* Jason Ryker. The one that, for reasons she may never understand, he refused to let anyone see.

But then someone cleared their throat, breaking whatever spell they'd both been in. In an instant, the hardened Agent was back, replacing the man kept hidden behind his thick, impenetrable walls.

Moving almost simultaneously, Jason stepped away while she let her hand drop back down to her side. Remembering where they were, Sophie looked to Christine to make sure she was okay, but the other woman was too busy staring slack jawed at something over Sophie's shoulder.

Or rather, some*one*.

She turned to see three of R.I.S.C.'s Alpha Team members standing just inside the doorway. She smiled, recognizing them immediately.

Jake McQueen, Grant Hill, and Sean "Coop" Cooper were all dressed in the same black combat gear as Jason. They wore helmets and night-vision similar in style to the ones Master Chief Warren had on, each holding their own M4 rifles.

And they were all looking back at the man standing next to her as if they weren't quite sure what to think.

Join the club.

"Jake?" Sophie shook her head in awe as she made her way around the foot of the bed and into the other man's arms.

"Hey, Soph." Her friend's husband hugged her back. "Glad you're okay."

Jake wasn't just married to her friend. He was also the company's owner and leader of R.I.S.C.'s Alpha Team.

R.I.S.C., which stood for Rescue, Intel, Security, and Capture, was the most elite private security agency in the country.

Olivia, Jake's wife, was the lead emergency nurse at the same private hospital where Sophie worked. The two had become close friends over the past couple of years.

Sophie had also treated more than one member of R.I.S.C., as well as helping to save Grant's wife when she was shot and nearly died. So she had gotten to know the team and their spouses pretty well.

Olivia's going to flip her shit when she finds out what happened.

After having been kidnapped and almost sold into sex slavery while on a medical mission trip two years ago, Olivia had made a new life with Jake and their adorable one-year-old daughter, Lily.

She and Sophie had talked in length about this trip before she'd left for Djibouti. And while Olivia understood and even supported Sophie's decision to come here, it was clear the other woman was worried for her.

"Did Liv send you to get me?" she asked Jake point blank.

The handsome former Delta Force operator chuckled. "Not directly. Although, when I told her I was coming here, she did order me to bring you back in one piece or else."

"Or else, what?"

Jake shrugged. "I guess we'll never know since that's exactly what we intend to do."

"I can't believe you all came." She looked at the badass black ops security team. "Thank you!"

"Don't thank us. Thank Ryker. He's the reason we're here." Jake tipped his chin to the man standing behind her.

Sophie swung around, her eyes finding Jason's. "You arranged all this?"

"My office received intel about a possible uprising in the area. I was given a list of American volunteers serving here. I saw your name, and I—"

"Speaking of gettin' outta here," Coop interjected. He nodded toward the bodies on the floor. "We should probably get a move on before their buddies decide to show up."

"There are more?" Christine stepped over the body of the man who'd nearly killed them and came to stand by Sophie's side.

"There are always more," Jason muttered emotionlessly as he also joined the group.

Sophie's mind was reeling. She wanted to ask him what he'd meant when he'd said that about seeing her name on the list. Surely, he hadn't come all this way solely because of her. Had he?

Don't be ridiculous.

Just then, McKenna "Mac" Kelley—the only female member of R.I.S.C.—poked her head in the door. "The other SEALs are here. We should be good for exfil."

"Exfil?" Sophie instinctively looked to Jason for an explanation.

"Exfiltrate. It means we're getting the hell out of here."

"Thank God." Christine exhaled loudly. "For a second, there, I really thought we were goners."

For a second there, so did she.

Out in the hallway, she saw the rest of Alpha Team. Next to Mac was Derek West, the team's computer genius, and Trevor Matthews, Jake's former Delta Force teammate.

With Jason hovering closely beside her, yet being careful not to touch her, Sophie and Christine followed the men and Mac down the hallway. Away from the carnage.

"Wait." Sophie stopped suddenly. Her gaze fell upon the entire group as she asked, "What about Master Chief Warren? He was in the stairwell heading to the first floor."

"Yeah." Christine nodded. "He held these men off so we could get away and hide."

The team's matching expression said it all.

Oh, no.

"He didn't make it, did he?" Sophie's eyes welled as she turned to Jason.

With his jaw tight, he shook his head. "Master Chief Warren gave his life for his country."

No, he'd given his life to save her and Christine.

Her heart ached for the brave man who'd lost everything to protect two women he didn't even know. "What about his team?" Sophie swiped at a stray tear. "He said they were in the building, too."

"They were," Jake confirmed. "We sent them out with the rest of your volunteer group so they could get them to safety."

"And Mr. Warren?" Christine asked quietly.

Jason looked at her and said, "He's with them."

Once outside the building, Sophie and Christine were shuffled into one of two armored SUVs. The team split up, half in one vehicle, half in the other.

Jason chose the seat beside her.

Other than the muffled sounds of a city being destroyed, the trip out of the city was fairly quiet. In fact, it wasn't until they parked the car at the Djibouti International Airport that Sophie finally spoke up.

"Now what?"

Jason turned to her and said, "Now, we go home."

Chapter 2

"You gonna tell me what the fuck that was all about?"

Jason looked up from his laptop, surprised to see Jake McQueen sitting in the seat beside him. He'd been so lost in his thoughts, he hadn't even noticed the guy walking up.

"What?"

"You know what."

Working damn hard not to react, he went back to the report he hadn't really been working on. "If I knew, I wouldn't have asked."

Before he could stop him, Jake's hand snaked out and slammed the computer shut, barely missing Jason's fingertips in the process.

"What the hell, McQueen?"

"Good." The cocky bastard smiled. "Now your focus is on me."

"Narcissistic much?" He lifted a brow.

Matching him, Jake shot back with, "Avoiding much?"

There was a slight pause before Jason flipped his computer open again and started typing. "I'm not avoiding shit, asshole. I'm trying to put a dent in the mound of paperwork I now have thanks to this op."

"An op *you* requested to join. Why was that, again?"

Ignore the smug bastard.

"Oh, that's right." Jake snapped his fingers and continued on. "Our mutual friend was in danger."

His back teeth ground together. "An entire group of American volunteers was in danger, Jake."

"True." Coop looked over the seat in front of him to join in on the conversation. "But there was only one volunteer you went batshit over."

"Fuck you, Coop. I didn't go batshit over anyone."

"Uh, yeah." The former Ranger smirked. "You kinda did."

With an exaggerated sigh, Jason shut the computer once more. Jesus, these guys were worse than a bunch of junior high pricks at the fucking lunch table.

"The woman was half a second away from having a bullet in her brain." A thought that still made him sick to his stomach. "Of course, I wanted to make sure she was okay."

"Come on, Ryker." Jake shot him a look that said he was full of shit. "It's okay to admit you like her."

Coop nodded. "Yeah, man. Lord knows we've all been there."

"I don't fucking like her, okay?" *Liar, liar, ass on fire.*

Shit. Had he spoken as loudly as it sounded? With a quick glance over his shoulder, Jason was relieved to see Sophie still asleep in her seat located at the back of the aircraft.

Just in case, he lowered his voice before turning back to the two annoying assholes. "She's a woman who works at my agency's hospital. Of course, I felt responsible for her. But on a purely professional level."

Those flames are getting bigger with every bullshit word you utter.

"A woman you hand-picked to work there, if memory serves me correctly."

Fuck me.

Of course Jake would remember that bit of information. Jason had only told the man that back when he was trying to convince Olivia to come work at Homeland's hospital, too.

Now McQueen was using it as ammunition for his adolescent antics.

"Fine," he conceded. "Yes, I hand-picked Sophie. She's a brilliant doctor who aced the interviews, and she came highly recommended. No, there isn't anything going on between us. And in case I've never made it clear to you in the past, my personal life is none of your goddamn business. Now, if the two of you will excuse me, I need to use the restroom."

"The restroom, huh?" Coop glanced down the aisle toward the back. "Would that be the same restroom that's close to where our lovely doctor is currently sitting?"

"It's the only restroom on the damn plane, dickwad." Jason stood. Setting his computer in his seat, he nudged Jake's leg. "You gonna move, or you want me to piss all over your lap."

"Gross." Jake scowled as he stood to get out of the way. "Damn, you're cranky when you're wrong."

"I'm not... " He sighed. "Forget it." With a shake of his head, he turned and started down the plane's narrow aisle.

Passing by the other AMOVA volunteers, Jason noticed that some of them were sleeping like babies while others seemed amped up from the day's events.

Everyone reacted to stress and danger differently. They'd no doubt have a few nightmares after this, but at least they were safe and heading back home.

All except one.

He thought about Colton Moore, the journalist who was officially listed as missing. Before leaving the hospital in Djibouti, Alpha Team had tried and failed to locate him.

Even the second group of SEALs that had arrived shortly after they'd saved Sophie and Christine had found no signs of the missing man.

Others were out looking for Moore, covering the streets of Djibouti and the surrounding area. But given the state of unrest the city was in, the man had probably gone underground to keep himself out of harm's way.

It would most likely take days, or even weeks to find him. But they'd keep looking. No way would they knowingly leave a United States citizen on his own in a situation like that.

Once inside the miniscule bathroom, Jason locked the door and turned on the faucet. He didn't actually need to go, he'd just used it as an excuse to get away from Jake and Coop's Spanish Inquisition.

All because he didn't want to see Sophie hurt.

So the fuck what? There wasn't a man on this jet that would stand by while some chicken shit bastard assaulted an innocent woman.

That man wasn't just assaulting her. He was going to kill her.

The image of the bastard's gun moving toward his Sophie was a sight he'd never forget.

She's not yours, dumbass.

No, she wasn't. He'd only spent the last four years *wishing* she was his while doing everything in his power to stay clear of her so she wouldn't know the truth.

A truth that he refused to fully admit to himself, let alone those jackasses out there.

Cupping his hands under the running faucet, Jason splashed the cold water over his face. He repeated the move twice more before drying his face with one of the clean hand towels in the built-in cabinet to his right.

Tossing it into the small hamper beneath the sink, he grabbed hold of the ceramic bowl's edge and locked his elbows. Staring at his reflection, he noticed a few silver hairs scattered throughout his temples and beard.

Jesus, man. When the hell did you get so old?

At thirty-eight, he knew he wasn't actually *old*. But damn if he didn't feel as though he was, most days.

The responsibility of holding people's lives in his hands on a daily basis took its toll on a person. Body, mind, and soul. And he'd been shouldering that responsibility for over half a decade.

Granted, he and his unit had saved many more lives than they'd lost—much with the help of R.I.S.C. But being the one to make the call on who goes where and when…that shit wears on you after a while.

At least it had him.

For a minute there, Jason almost crossed the point of no return. He'd gotten so caught up in the end game, he'd damn near lost sight of the very thing that had driven him to do this job in the first place.

The phrase 'for the greater good' had been so ingrained in him, he'd become blinded to the other lives that were affected by the choices he made and the plans he put into action.

Like the choice he'd made years before. The one that had cost him his entire fucking future.

Maybe that's why he felt the need to personally intervene with this rescue mission. Maybe that's why he had such a strong, almost overwhelming urge to be hands-on with the rescue of one of his people. Maybe that's why—

You know exactly why you wanted to tag along with Jake and the others. And she's sitting right outside this door.

He met his own gaze once more and he knew. That damn voice was right...again.

Though they had nothing more than a cordial, professional relationship, Jason had wanted to be the one to find her and bring her home. No, he'd *needed* to be the one.

Because when it came to Sophia Ruiz, he didn't trust anyone else to keep her safe.

There was a knock on the door followed by Derek's southern voice. "You 'bout done in there, Ryker? You didn't fall in, did ya?"

Pushing away from the sink, Jason opened the door and stepped into the small area just outside the restroom. "It's all yours."

"Thanks, man." Derek moved past him quickly. "Drank too much damn Gatorade. My bladder's about to burst."

"Didn't need to know that, but okay."

With a grin, the other man shut the door as Jason turned to head back to his seat. He glanced down at Sophie, expecting her to still be asleep. Instead those brown eyes of hers were looking straight at him.

"Hey," he muttered low.

Smooth, Jason. Really smooth.

Sitting up a little straighter, she adjusted the thin blanket he'd found in one of the compartments when they'd boarded.

"Hey." Her lips curved into a smile that didn't come close to reaching her eyes.

Her smiles can light up an entire room. They should always, always *reach her fucking eyes.*

"How you holdin' up?"

"Okay." She forced another non-smile before letting it fall flat. "Actually, that's a lie."

"What's wrong?" Concern for her had him dropping into the empty seat next to her. "Are you hurting? I can get Trevor to get you something more for pain if you—"

"No, I'm not in pain." She shook her head. "Not really. I mean, my ribs and face are sore, but it's nothing I can't handle. I just...I keep seeing that man. That *gun*." Sophie cleared her throat. "I really thought he was going to kill me."

"I'm sorry you had to go through that."

"At least the shaking finally stopped." Sophie grinned, holding out a hand to back up her claim.

"That's good." Jason offered her a small smile. "Adrenaline dumps can be a real bitch."

"Yeah, I'm definitely not a fan."

He'd felt her tremors earlier, in the SUV. It had taken everything he had not to haul her into his lap and comfort her until they stopped.

As soon as they'd gotten onto the jet, Jason had asked Trevor to look Sophie over. As a former Delta Force operator and Alpha Team's medic, he felt confident in the other man's training and abilities.

After a quick field exam, Trevor had reported she had some bruised ribs from being shoved against the bed's metal railing—her words—and her cheek wasn't broken, but had begun to turn fifty shades of purple.

Though she didn't complain about them, Sophie also had bruises beginning to form on the skin covering her neck.

Rage gripped its meaty claws around his heart. It was bad enough the bastard had struck her and damn near killed her, but he'd also choked her at some point, too?

I want to go back and kill the son of a bitch all over again. Slowly.

"Are *you* okay?" Sophie looked back at him with concern.

It was only then that Jason realized his fists were white knuckled in his lap. Shit. He needed to get himself together and act like the government agent he was.

"I'm good," he lied. "Just glad we got there when we did."

"Me, too." She shuddered. "If you'd been two seconds later..."

Sophie didn't finish the sentence, but she didn't have to. They both knew exactly what would've happened had he and the others arrived any later than they had.

"You said you're not okay." He watched her closely. "Is it just the flashbacks, or something more?"

"I'm just...I don't know." Focusing on a loose thread hanging from the blanket's edge, she said, "I just can't believe everything that happened. The destruction in the city...poor Master Chief Warren. And then there's Colton." Sophie's eyes returned to his. "Have you heard anything more about him?"

"Not yet, but we're still looking. And we're going to *keep* looking until we find him."

Her expression was unreadable. "That man...the one you shot. Do you know who he was?"

Jason wondered what she thought after having witnessed him taking a man's life. Was she repulsed? Did she see him as damaged goods?

Questions like those had never mattered to him before. Neither had the answers. But now, with her, *everything* seemed to matter.

Much more than it probably should.

"The man who attacked you was Abdul Qasim," he answered her question. "He was the head of Alhukkam, a Yemeni extremists group who led the attack in Djibouti."

Jason had recognized him the second he saw his dead body lying at Sophie's feet. Thanks to reliable chatter, Abdul had been on Homeland's radar for a while, now.

"Why would he—"

"I don't have all the details yet," he cut her off. "But I do know Abdul had known ties to a Yemini nationalist group."

Sophie took a moment to process this before sharing, "He...he was looking for Colton."

The same Colton who was now missing.

Jason perked up at that. "Abdul? What did he want with Moore?"

"I don't know." She shrugged a shoulder, causing the blanket to slip down a few inches. "He wanted me to call him."

"And did you?"

"No."

Probably why the asshole hit her.

"Why not?"

"I knew if I called him, I'd be sending Colton into a trap."

She said it so matter-of-factly. As if that brave, crazy decision hadn't damn near cost her her life.

Jason ran a hand over his beard, speaking with a slow and steady tone. "By not calling him, you ran the risk of getting yourself and the woman who was with you killed."

"I know." She bit her bottom lip. "I just...I couldn't do it."

If he hadn't fallen for the woman when they first met, Jason would've gone head over boots in that very instant.

She'd risked her life...was willing to *sacrifice* herself...to save a man she hardly knew.

That knowledge made him want to pull her into his arms and never let her go. It also made him want to put her over his knee.

Of course, if she had called Moore, Qasim would've just shot her and her fellow volunteer afterward.

Sophie had been put into an impossible position and had made the only decision she could live with.

God, she was incredible.

"What happens now?" Her weary eyes met his.

"When we land, you'll all be taken to my building so you can give your official statements about what happened. You'll be separated, but only to ensure your memories of the events that took place aren't skewed by something someone else says."

He needed her to understand that. The last thing he wanted her thinking was that she was in some sort of trouble over what happened.

"Will you be there?" She asked almost hesitantly. "When I'm being questioned, I mean?"

Does she want me there?

He shook his head. "Because I was actively involved in the op, another agent will be assigned to take your statement. But I promise, I won't be far if you need something."

"Okay." Disappointment flickered behind her chocolate eyes.

She does want me there.

The primal male in him wanted to do a fist pump. The Federal agent in him kept his cool and didn't react.

"I'm not going to lie, it's probably going to take at least a couple of hours to get everything sorted out. But after that, you'll be free to go."

"I understand." She nodded. "I just hope you hear something about Colton soon. I'm really worried about him."

Was she worried because he was an acquaintance, or something more? Unfamiliar jealousy started to seep into his veins as he began to wonder if she and the journalist had become romantically involved.

He actually opened his mouth to ask her when the phone in his pocket began to vibrate. Pulling it out, he saw that it was one of the select few people within the agency that were higher on the pay scale than he was.

"I'm sorry." He stood and turned to Sophie. "I have to take this."

"Of course."

With the phone still vibrating in his hand, he spared another second to tell her, "You're one of the strongest women I've ever met, Soph. You're going to be just fine."

Though her skin wasn't at all pale, he could still make out the slight flush rising into her cheeks. He suddenly found himself standing there, wondering if she looked that way when she made love.

Not the time, asshole. Not. The. Time.

The silent ringing on his phone ceased. Damn it. He really needed to return that call ASAP. So why wasn't he walking away?

When the call came through again, it kicked his ass in gear. "We still have a few hours before we land," he informed her. "Try to get some rest."

"I will."

Turning to leave, he took a single step before a delicate hand grabbed his, stopping him in his tracks.

"Jason?"

Ignoring the electric burn her touch created, he turned back around. "Yeah?"

"You saved my life." Her voice cracked, but she cleared it and continued on. "I know it's not enough, but...thank you."

Momentarily forgetting the call, Jason gave her hand a gentle squeeze. "You don't ever have to thank me for that, sweetheart."

Then, before he did something monumentally crazy like pull her out of that seat and into his arms, he released her hand and walked away, answering the phone as he went.

Chapter 3

"For the millionth time, Liv...I'm *fine*." Sophie lifted her bottle of water and put its rim to her lips.

Three weeks had passed since the incident in Djibouti, and everyone she knew still acted like they were waiting for her to break. Some moments she felt as though she would, but for the most part, she really did feel as though she was handling it all okay.

"And for the millionth time, I'm calling bullshit." Sitting across from her at their usual table in the hospital cafeteria, Olivia McQueen shot her a pointed look. "This is me you're talking to, remember? I'm like the poster child for this sort of thing."

The comment made Sophie snort. "Sorry. I shouldn't laugh..."

"Oh, no. It's quite comical." The other woman shook her head, her brown ponytail swishing back and forth with the movement. "After Jake and his team rescued me, this one organization contacted me. They *literally* wanted to put my picture on a poster with the words 'Volunteer Violence Awareness' at the top in big, block letters."

Sophie felt her mouth drop. "They didn't."

"Oh, but they did."

"What did you say?"

"I politely told them thanks, but no thanks." Liv took a drink of her coffee, taking her time before getting the conversation back on track. "Okay, look. I'm not trying to hound you. I promise, I'm not. But did you at least call Dr. Heller?"

"I did, actually." Sophie nodded. "I have an appointment with her in two days."

Dr. Monica Heller was a local counseling psychologist. She specialized in working with those who'd fallen victim to violence, specifically survivors of abduction and/or murder attempts.

When Sophie and the others first returned home from Djibouti, Olivia had reached out almost immediately. Having survived much worse than what Sophie had gone through, the sweet nurse had wanted to make sure she was okay, and knew she wasn't alone in the aftermath.

Yes, some days were difficult, and more often than not, her nights were still sleepless. But she'd done what she always did when life got tough...she pushed through it.

Getting back to work helped more than anything. She was back to having a normal routine, and the job kept her mind occupied on other things.

It was when she was alone, and the shadows of the night crept in...those were the moments she felt afraid and vulnerable.

"You're going to love Monica." Olivia broke through her thoughts. "She's not pushy or overbearing. She really listens and...well, anyway." She waved herself off. "I'm just glad you're going to see her. But there's no pressure, here. If you don't think she's a good fit, let me know and I'll help you find someone who is. And don't forget, you can always come to me. Night or day."

Sophie's heart felt full as she stared back at her hazel-eyed friend. "Thanks, Liv. I know it probably feels like I'm blowing you off, but I'm not. I really do appreciate all you've done since I got back."

"What are friends for?" Olivia smiled. "And speaking of friends, Jake said Ryker seemed overly interested in becoming one of yours. Said the guy went apeshit when he saw that man trying to hurt you."

A sudden spike in her pulse took Sophie off guard, her body reacting to just the mention of the man's name.

"Jake's exaggerating," she brushed it off. "Jason was just doing his job. Nothing more."

"Huh." Olivia took another sip of coffee. "Well, *Jason* must be doing a damn thorough job seeing as how he's been here five times in the last two weeks. Not to mention, he's just happened to run into you *all* five times."

"I didn't realize you were keeping track." Okay, so maybe she had been, too. But Sophie had tried not to read too much into it. "The man helps run this place, Liv. Of course, he's going to be here occasionally."

"Occasionally, sure." The other woman nodded. "Just seems like his *occasions* have occurred more frequently since you guys got back. And the way he looks at you when he's here?" Olivia fanned herself dramatically.

Sophie's heart thumped hard against her ribs even as she muttered, "Whatever."

"Come on, Soph. Are you really going to tell me you haven't noticed?"

Oh, she'd noticed. She'd also convinced herself it was all in her head. Wishful thinking and all that.

"I'm sure he's checked in on all the volunteers. Probably part of his job description or something."

"Uh...no." Olivia's face twisted. "Pretty sure that's not it."

"Yeah, well, it doesn't matter. Even if he was interested...which he's not...he hasn't said a word about it."

"Because men are idiots when it comes to women."

She had a point, but still, "Yours seems to do all right in that department."

"Are you kidding?" Olivia chuckled. "It took that man a full ten *years* before he finally admitted his true feelings for me."

"Yeah, but from what you've said, *you* hadn't told him how you felt, either. Right?"

"You're right." Olivia shook her head and sighed. "I guess we were both pretty stupid. So maybe I'm not the best person to give romantic advice, after all. You know what? Next time I try to interfere with your love life, feel free to tell me to butt out."

Sophie's gaze narrowed on the other woman's. "So, if I told you to mind your own business and step off, you would?"

Olivia thought for a moment then grinned. "Nah. I'd probably ignore you and keep trying anyway."

"Because that's the kind of friend you are?"

With a chuckle, Olivia smiled wide. "Exactly."

The two women laughed as they stood and grabbed their drinks. They were only halfway through their day and needed to get back to the ER before the patients started piling up.

"Hey, ladies. Looks like you two are enjoying your break."

The familiar voice had both women turning their heads. Sophie's breath stuttered when she saw him.

Dressed in a dark blue suit and white button up, Jason looked every bit the government agent he was. And damn, if her insides didn't ignite.

"Hey, Jason." Olivia's tone was a bit overzealous. "We were just talking about you."

Sophie shot her friend a look.

Why? Why would she say that?

"Really?" The sexy man slid his hands into his pockets, one corner of his tempting mouth curving slightly. "Should I be concerned?"

"Not at all." Sophie offered him a quick smile. "We were just talking about what happened in Africa and how well you handled yourself over there."

Nice cover, Ruiz.

"That's right," Olivia followed her cue. "Jake said it was almost as if you were part of the team."

"Djibouti wasn't my first run-in with guys like Qasim," he commented. "But it was nice to know I had Jake and the others by my side this go-around."

An awkward stretch of silence passed before Olivia finally spoke up again. "Okay, then. I'd better get back to the E.R. before the next shift change." She looked at Sophie. "You coming?"

"Actually"—Jason intervened—"I'd like to talk to Soph for a minute, if that's okay?" His eyes were on Sophie's. "It won't take long."

"Oh, um...sure." Sophie nodded. "Liv can page me if they need me. Right, Liv?"

"Of course." Olivia gave her a knowing grin. "I'll catch you two kids later. Good to see you again, Jason."

"You, too." Jason tipped his chin.

Not sure what it was he wanted to discuss with her, Sophie waited for him to begin the conversation.

As soon as Olivia was out of earshot, he surprised the hell out of her when he asked, "Would you like grab a bite to eat after your shift?"

Holy shit. Was he actually asking her out on a date?

"There are some things I wanted to run by you," he clarified. "Just a few follow-up questions, is all. With our busy schedules, I thought we could knock out a meal while we went over them."

So...*not* a date.

Being careful not to let her disappointment show, Sophie offered him a smile. "Sure. Dinner's fine. My shift ends at seven. Just give me time to run home and clean up, and I can meet you wherever. Is eight-thirty too late?"

Because date or not, she'd definitely want to take a shower and change first.

"Eight-thirty's fine. And I can pick you up, if that's okay? I have a meeting downtown at six-thirty, so I'll be driving past your neighborhood, anyway."

Sophie blinked.

He knows where I live?

Then it hit her. Of course, he knew her address. It was printed at the top of the resume she'd given him four years ago, and she hadn't moved since.

And even if he didn't have it filed away somewhere, the guy worked for Homeland. For him, finding out where she lived would be child's play.

"In that case, I'll be ready by eight-thirty."

"Great." His lips curved into an almost-smile. "I'll see you, then."

"See you, then."

As she watched him walk away—and damn, what a sight that was—Sophie took the next few minutes to figure out exactly what had just happened.

She was going out to dinner with Jason Ryker. Man of her dreams. Star of her fantasies.

But not as a date. As an informal interrogation with food.

Better than nothing, right?

Heading back to the ER, Sophie couldn't help but wonder what sort of questions he could have for her. The incident in Djibouti happened weeks ago, and she'd already told him and the other agents everything she knew.

Maybe this is about Colton.

Had they finally found the missing journalist? The thought nearly made her steps faulter.

Every media outlet available had been running his story non-stop. They'd even compared it Olivia's tragic experience two years prior when she'd gone missing and was presumed dead.

The hope was that Colton's story would end the same way Liv's had. That he'd be found alive, rescued, and brought back home in one piece.

But the more Sophie thought about it, the more she realized Jason wouldn't have kept something like that from her. He would've told her if Colton had been found. Even if the news wasn't good.

It doesn't take an entire dinner to tell a person someone's dead.

The remainder of her shift seemed to drag on forever. Despite her efforts against it, Sophie's mind kept running through scenario after scenario, trying desperately to come up with what information Jason was looking to gain.

She didn't tell Olivia about the impromptu dinner slash question session, but only because the woman would no doubt make it into something it wasn't.

Sophie would fill her in later, after she found out exactly what Jason wanted from her.

Too bad it's not what you want from him.

When seven o'clock rolled around, Sophie handed her patients off to the next doctor, skirted out of the hospital, and took the shortcut home to give herself plenty of time to get ready.

This may not be a romantic dinner, but that didn't mean she couldn't still make herself look nice.

By eight-fifteen, she was dressed and ready to go. She didn't know where he planned to take her, but since he was wearing a suit, she'd chosen a casual dress.

The cross-pleated dress was sleeveless and form-fitting, but loose enough to be comfortable. It was dark gray, so not the little black dress one she'd normally pick, and its bottom hem stopped two inches above her knees.

With her dark hair pulled half-up, Sophie had left the bottom section of her soft curls free to fall down to the center of her back.

She'd gone a little bolder with her makeup than was her norm, but nothing too excessive. The smoky look on her eyes was a bit much for the ER, but perfectly acceptable for a night out.

To top the look off, Sophie had chosen a pair of blush-colored heels. The lighter-toned shoes helped to visually elongate her short stature, and at five-three, she needed all the help she could get.

Giving herself a final once-over in the floor-length mirror in her bedroom. She spun around slowly, checking every angle the handsome agent would see.

To her, she appeared sexy yet modest. Casual, yet dressy. The question was, what would Jason think when he saw her?

This isn't a date, remember? Not. A. Date.

Her brain knew and even understood that fact, but the butterflies twirling around in her stomach had yet to receive the message.

At eight-twenty-eight, the doorbell rang. Her stomach tensed.

He's here.

Forcing a casual expression, Sophie flipped off her bedroom light and went downstairs. Grabbing her clutch purse and pashmina, both matching her shoes, she went to her door and reached for the knob.

Drawing in a deep, calming breath, she released it slowly before opening the door with a smile.

"Right on time. Impressive."

"Wow." Jason blinked, his eyes traveling the length of her body and up again. "You clean up nicely, Doc."

"Thanks. I'd say the same for you, but you're always cleaned up when I see you."

Except for Africa. When he'd come for her that day, he'd looked like an alpha badass in his black combat gear.

Her insides clenched at the memory.

It was probably inappropriate for her to be turned on by memories of him minutes after he'd taken another man's life. But she couldn't seem to help it.

Should probably put that on my list of things to discuss with Dr. Heller.

But what would she tell the therapist?

Should she explain that, dressed in his everyday suit and tie, Jason Ryker was the epitome of the sexiest suit porn in existence? Or that seeing him in action with Jake and the others had sparked even more fantasies about the closed-off agent than the ones she'd already created?

Fantasies that kept her up at night, even when the monsters didn't.

Clearing his throat. "Shall we?" He motioned toward his car, which was parked behind hers in her driveway.

Afraid to speak just then, Sophie turned and locked the door before walking beside Jason as they made their way to his car.

In her mind, she imagined him placing his hand on her lower back as they moved. She could almost feel the heat from his palm searing into her skin there.

But he didn't touch her at all because, as she had to keep reminding herself, this wasn't a freaking date.

Even so, he opened the car door for her like a gentleman before rounding the car and sliding behind the wheel. His car smelled of leather and spice. The leather from the expensive upholstery, and the familiar spice from the man sitting beside her.

The drive was filled with small talk about the damp spring weather and how her day at the hospital had gone.

It was clear he wasn't going to get into the meat of why he'd wanted them to meet up until after they got to wherever they were going. So she didn't bother to ask.

The way she saw it, if they didn't start that conversation until dinner, the evening might last a little longer than if they delved into it all now.

Wow. Pathetic, much?

It wasn't like Sophie never dated. She'd even dated the same guy more than once a few times.

She was just very particular about who she agreed to go out with, and even more picky about who she went to bed with.

The fact was, she refused to settle for anything less than what she wanted. What she knew she deserved.

Growing up, she'd witnessed what a loveless marriage looked like. The yelling. The deafening silence.

The hitting.

Sophie had read all the statistics. She knew how common it was for girls growing up in that kind of environment to end up choosing men who treated them the same way.

Screw that.

For as long as she could remember, she'd promised herself to never end up like her mother. While she didn't understand it, she didn't fault her mom for loving her father.

The heart wants what it wants.

The old cliché was a cliché for a reason.

Sophie thought of the man sitting beside her. Was he the one her heart wanted? Maybe.

Her body, however, had absolutely no doubt about what—or who—it wanted.

With most guys, it was pretty clear from the first couple of dates whether or not they were going to fit the bill. If not, she saw no reason to waste either of their times by dragging out a losing game.

In the past, Olivia and the other RISC wives had commented that she was too picky. That maybe her standards were a tad high. And maybe they were right.

Didn't change the fact that she'd rather be alone than with someone who didn't make her happy.

Bright lights pulled her away from her thoughts when Jason pulled the car into a well-lit parking lot. She glanced up and saw that he'd brought her to her favorite restaurant...The Gardens.

"I love this place." She perked up. "Did you know it's owned by Lexi Matthews, Trevor's wife?" The same Trevor that was Jake's SIC, or second in charge on Alpha Team.

"I did." Jason put the car in park. "Glad to know I chose well."

She looked at him like he was nuts. "Uh, *well* is an understatement. I mean, I've only eaten here a handful of times, but I swear, Lexi makes the best food in the state."

"Agreed." A ghost of a smile reached his lips.

Suddenly famished, Sophie didn't wait for him to come around before getting out of the car and shutting the door behind her. A cool breeze blew past, so she wrapped the soft pashmina around her shoulders as she and Jason made their way to the restaurant's entrance.

"You heard about what happened here a while back, right?" Sophie knew he probably did, but she needed to talk about *something*. "This past Valentine's Day when those men tried to rob the place?"

"I did." Jason nodded. "I was out of the country when it happened, but I found out about it when I got back."

"Thank God Lexi wasn't hurt. I wasn't working the day it happened, but Olivia was. She said Lexi had just found out she was pregnant not long before that. I know our situations were different, but I can't imagine how much worse it would've been for me had I been pregnant on top of it all."

A look crossed over Jason's face, but it was gone before Sophie could decipher what it meant.

Opening one of the two large, wooden doors, he waited for her to enter the establishment first before following her inside. Though it was well past 'normal' dinnertime, the place was still buzzing with activity.

"Good evening, Mr. Ryker," the young hostess greeted them. "Your table is ready. If you'll follow me…"

Sophie's brows rose as they fell in line behind the other woman. "Wow." She grinned. "You must come here a lot if they know your name."

"I've eaten here a few times." He shrugged.

All of a sudden, Sophie found herself wondering how many other women he'd brought here before her. Not that it mattered, since their evening was about business and not pleasure.

Except for some reason, it did matter. Much more than it should.

Once they were seated, their server came back to take their drink orders. With her nod of approval, Jason ordered them each a glass of wine, as well as some ice water.

More than ready to find out what this was all about, Sophie waited for the gentleman to leave and then asked point blank, "What is it you want to know?"

"Straight to the point. I like that."

So did she, which explained why the vagueness with which he'd approached this evening was driving her crazy.

Sophie folded her hands on top of her menu and waited. Jason's mouth twitched as if he were fighting a smile, but then he cleared his throat and got down to business.

"Like I said when we spoke at the hospital, I just had a few follow-up questions for you."

"Okay, shoot."

"Mainly, I wanted to know if there was anything else you could remember. Something you saw in the days leading up to the attack, or maybe something Qasim or one of the other men said. Either to you or his men."

"I'm sorry." She shook her head. "I've told you everything I know."

He nodded. "Okay."

A stretch of silence passed before Sophie asked, "Have you heard anything about Colton?"

"Unfortunately, no. For the most part, the violent activity in Djibouti has begun to subside, but—"

"Here you go." Their server chose that moment to return with their wine. "Are you ready to order, or do you need more time?"

Jason looked to her for the answer.

"I'm ready." She nodded. To the server she said, "I'd like a half portion of the pasta primavera with shrimp instead of chicken, please."

"And for your side?"

"A house salad, light dressing."

"Excellent choice. And for you, sir?"

Jason ordered a medium-rare steak, baked potato, and salad, the combination making her smile.

His dark brows furrowed just a smidge when their server left. "What?"

"Nothing." Sophie waved it off.

"Tell me."

When he spoke like that, his voice all deep and rumbly, it made Sophie think she would do or say anything he wanted.

Preferably in the bedroom.

Nearly choking on the thought, she told him, "I was just thinking if I had to order for you, those are the exact choices I would've gone with."

His dark, rugged beard lifted with a grin. "Why is that?"

Sophie chuckled, admitting, "I have no idea."

"Good instincts, would be my guess."

"Maybe." She took a sip of the delicious vino, the combination of sweet and tart notes crossing over her tastebuds perfectly. "This is delicious. Nice choice."

"Guess I have good instincts, as well."

Their eyes met, her heart beating a little harder. "I guess you do."

For a moment, the two remained like that...staring back at each other as if they were the only two people in the room. But then the salads and complimentary bread were delivered, cutting the entrancing moment short.

"So." Jason stabbed a piece of lettuce with his fork. "Back to what I was saying. We've had a few leads on Moore over the past few weeks, but so far, nothing has panned out."

Moving the crisp green leaves around her plate, Sophie shook her head. "I don't understand. One minute, he was right there in the staff lounge with Christine and me. The next, he'd just...vanished."

"Did he say anything weird or out of the ordinary? Was he acting suspicious at all or give you any reason to stop and take pause?"

"No." She set her fork down. "The head of the department came and told us the US Navy was sending a team in to get us out of the building and onto safe ground. He said we were to gather our things, find a room, and stay there until we were found."

All things she'd mentioned in her official statement.

"So why wasn't Colton with you and Christine in that room?"

Sophie thought back to that day. She pictured those last moments just before they left the lounge.

"His head was hurting."

"What do you mean?" Jason leaned his elbows onto the table. "Was he injured?"

"No." She shook her head. "He had a headache. I just remembered that part. He said he woke up with it that morning and it hadn't gotten any better. Then he asked if I had some ibuprofen he could take." Sophie found herself back in that moment. "I was helping Christine shove her things into her bag, so I told Colton to check mine. I get stress headaches sometimes, so I usually keep some ibuprofen there, just in case. But I wasn't sure if I had any left."

"And did you?"

"I don't know." She looked back at him. "One minute, I was helping Christine while he was looking through my things, and the next he said he needed to go check on something and he'd find us. I tried to..." Her voice broke. "I tried to stop him, but he didn't listen." His image started to blur, but she blinked the moisture away. "I should've tried harder."

"Hey." Jason reached across the table and covered her hand with his. "Whatever happened to him, that's not on you. He was a grown man who made the decision to leave. His choice."

"I know." Sophie sniffed, glancing down at their joined hands. "Logically, I know you're right. I mean, I've run through the scenario a thousand times. If Colton had been in that room, all three of us probably would've been killed. Either that or they would've killed Christine and I, and then taken him with them. Either way..."

"You're right." He didn't pull any punches. "You and Christine would both be dead, and Colton would either be dead or in the hands of terrorists."

"Just like he is, now."

"We don't know that." Jason brushed his thumb across the back of her hand. "There's also a third option."

Sophie looked back at him. "He could be hiding."

"That's right. He may have known those men were coming for him. If that was the case, then it's possible he went underground."

"But how would he have known? And why would they have been after him in the first place?"

"Both valid questions. Moore wasn't doing an investigative story like the ones he's done in the past. This one was supposed to be all about the good AMOVA was doing for the people of Djibouti."

"Exactly." Sophie nodded. "It doesn't make any sense. Unless..."

"Unless what?"

"Nothing." She hesitated to say. "Just my imagination running wild."

"Come on, Soph." There was that rumble again. "Tell me what you're thinking."

Most people called her Sophie. On occasion, Olivia or Jake called her Soph. But for some reason, when *this* man called her that, it made her insides tingle like a teenage girl with her first crush.

Get it together, Ruiz. You're a grown woman, for crying out loud.

"I was just thinking...what if we're wrong? What if Colton *was* investigating something we didn't know about? Something involving those men. What if they found out and that's why they went after him?"

"It's a great theory, but I've checked with all the other agencies. They all said the same thing...Colton Moore was not on their payroll when he left for Africa."

"Well, like I said...just my overactive imagination."

"We all considered that as a possible theory, Soph. Unfortunately, everything on that front has come up empty, as well."

"So we're back to he's either dead or he's being held against his will."

"Most likely, yes." He nodded.

"For his sake and that of his family, I hope he's at least still alive."

"So do I, sweetheart." He gave her hand a gentle squeeze. "So do I."

Chapter 4

Jason forced himself to keep his hands at his sides as he walked Sophie to her door. He wanted to reach for her. To place his hand on the small of her back.

To touch her again, even if it was in the smallest of ways.

When he'd held her hand, earlier, his intention had been to offer comfort. But just like when she'd grabbed his hand on the plane a few weeks ago, his entire body had felt the jolt from her touch.

Imagine what kissing her would be like.

He *had* been imagining it. All. Fucking. Night. Long.

"Thanks, again for dinner." She stopped in front of her door and faced him. "I know it was business, but I still had a really nice time."

"I did, too."

A stretch of thick, awkward silence passed between them.

Either kiss her or walk away.

Jason knew what he *wanted* to do. More than anything, he wanted to lean in, take her mouth in his, and finally taste what he'd been craving for the past four years.

But like the dumbass he was, he heard himself say, "I should probably go."

"Okay." Sophie gave him a little nod. "Goodnight, Jason."

"Goodnight, Sophie."

Forcing himself to turn away, he took a step to leave. But then he heard…

"Why did you ask me to dinner tonight?"

He faced her again. "What?"

She pulled the wrap covering her shoulders a little tighter. "Why did you really ask me to dinner?"

He swallowed the truth. "I told you. I had questions I needed to—"

"You could've asked those over the phone." She moved closer. "Or you could've asked them earlier, when we spoke in the cafeteria."

"I could have," he admitted.

"So why didn't you?"

Man up and tell her, asshole.

His chest tightened, his heart slamming against his ribs. "I think you know why."

"Maybe." Her enticing gaze remained locked with his. "But I'm a doctor, so I'm not big on making assumptions. Especially when it comes to men. Besides..." She inched forward. "Sometimes a girl needs to hear the words."

Jason studied her a moment. The hesitation hiding behind her playful flirting making him think maybe she'd been hurt in the past.

I'll hunt the bastard down and kill him.

"I asked you to dinner because I wanted to spend time with you outside the hospital walls."

There. Now she knew the truth.

The moonlight reflected off her gorgeous eyes, making it possible for him to notice the way her pupils expanded with his words. The corners of her plump lips curved into a slow smile.

"Was that so hard?" she asked quietly.

Baby, you have no idea.

A breeze blew some hair into her face, and before he thought better of it, Jason reached out and brushed the stray strands behind her ear.

Despite his earlier decision to leave, he stepped closer. Their bodies separated by mere inches.

With his heart trying to pound its way out of his chest, he brought his other hand up to frame her face and whispered, "You're so beautiful."

Raising a hand, Sophie wrapped her fingers around one of his thick wrists. She didn't say a word, just stared up at him as if she wanted nothing more than for him to kiss her.

He made life and death decisions damn near every single day. He had the President of the United States on speed dial, for fuck's sake. And he'd seen more war and destruction than most people could even imagine.

He'd lost everything in one horrific, life-altering moment.

But right now, in *this* moment, Jason was more terrified than he'd ever been in his entire life.

"Soph, I—"

"Kiss me."

Hell, yes!

He was not a man that needed to be told twice.

Leaning in, Jason pressed his lips to hers. Despite the sudden jolt to his system, he held back, fighting the urge to devour her right there on her front stoop.

He kept the kiss soft. Gentle. A light feathering as he took his time savoring the precious moment only a first kiss could bring.

Except this was already better than any kiss he'd ever experienced. And the best part was, they were just getting started.

Jason parted his lips, letting the tip of his tongue run along the seam of her soft and welcoming mouth. He sent up a silent prayer of thanks when Sophie opened up for him, eagerly inviting him in.

Their tongues met and passion ignited. A low grunt escaped from deep inside his chest when he got his first real taste, and he tilted their heads to allow him to get even closer.

Not close enough. It'll never be close enough.

His cock screamed to be let loose. It ached and throbbed, so full and demanding, it was damn near painful.

Sophie let out a tiny moan, the sound making his rock-solid dick jump behind his zipper. And when she clutched the lapels of his jacket between her small fists, Jason damn near lost all control.

He turned their bodies, pressing her back against her home's door, and his front against hers. On their own accord, his hips thrust forward, his body desperately searching for the release it knew this woman would bring.

Afraid he'd gone too far, Jason thought about pulling away. But at the exact same moment he began to move, Sophie rubbed her lower belly against his obvious erection.

She moaned again, damn near bringing him to his breaking point.

"Soph..." He panted against her mouth.

"Yeah?"

"We should stop."

"Why on earth would we do that?"

"Because, sweetheart." A low chuckle rolled through him as he used Herculean effort to pull back enough to look her in the eye. "If we don't stop now, we'll end up giving your neighbors a show they won't soon forget. And I don't intend to share you with anyone."

As if she'd just remembered where they were, Sophie blinked and slowly straightened her spine. "I suppose you're right." She thought for a moment and then, "I'd invite you in for a drink, but I'd just end up kissing you again."

And that's a problem because...

Because Jason didn't want this to turn into a one-night stand. No, he wanted more with this woman.

Much, *much* more.

"And if I came inside, I wouldn't want to stop at just kissing." He tucked a lock of hair behind her ear like before and smiled. "We'll get there, Soph. Just not tonight."

Relief mixed with the arousal swirling in the browns of her eyes. "Thanks for understanding."

He understood perfectly.

She wanted him, too. That was obvious the moment their lips first touched. But like him, she didn't want to rush whatever was happening between them.

Another burst of wind flew past, and though she was still flushed from their intimate moment, Jason saw the shiver racing down her spine.

Ignoring his protesting dick, he tipped his chin toward her door. "Go on. Before you catch a cold. And be sure to lock up."

A wide smile deepened her cute as fuck dimples. "Yes, Dad."

"Sorry." He ran a hand over his beard. "Occupational hazard."

"It's okay." She placed a palm over his racing heart. "It's nice to know you care."

In a moment of uncharacteristic admission, Jason told her, "I do care, Soph. A lot."

More than I've cared about anyone in a very long time.

The red in her cheeks grew darker, but she made his heart sore when she whispered back, "I do, too."

Rising up onto her tiptoes, Sophie closed her eyes and kissed him again. This one was short and sweet, but somehow even more intimate than the mind-blowing one they'd shared moments before.

"Goodnight, Jason," she whispered against his lips.

"Goodnight, sweetheart."

Jason watched while she unlocked her door and went inside. He waited for the telltale snick of the locks being engaged before turning and heading down the sidewalk.

There was a bounce in his step that hadn't been there in...forever. And a smile on his face that may never go away.

Climbing behind the wheel, he was already thinking of when they could go out again when he heard a loud *bang* coming from inside Sophie's home.

He'd heard the sound many times before. In the field...at the range. Someone had just shot a gun.

And that someone was inside with Sophie.

Fuck, no.

He was not going to lose her. Not now. Not like this.

Jason shot out of his car, pulling the Glock he always carried from his holster as he took off in a dead sprint. Leaping over the short set of concrete steps leading to Sophie's door, he heard a bloodcurdling scream that sounded a lot like his name.

A fraction of a second later, another gunshot blasted, turning his blood ice cold. A loud thud came from up above, making his fear spike to a nauseating level.

"*Sophia!*" he yelled as the heel of his dress shoe slammed into the wood just above the top lock. An explosion of splinters flew to the sides, but Jason ignored them and entered Sophie's home.

Spotting the staircase to his left, he ran as fast as his legs would move. Taking the steps two at a time, Jason made it to the top just in time to hear a set of heavy footfalls followed by the sound of glass shattering.

His stomach dropped. Jesus, had she just been shot and then thrown out a fucking window?

He followed the direction of the noise to the room at the end of the hall. Adrenaline pumped through his body, but he called upon his training as he approached the half-open door with caution.

Damn it, he wanted to barge in but going in blind and getting himself shot would do Sophie no good.

Taking precious seconds to stop and listen, he found the room quiet. *Eerily* quiet.

Terror for the woman he'd held in his arms minutes before threatened to take over, but he pushed it back. He pushed *everything* back except the primal need to protect her.

Keeping his weapon trained in front of him, Jason used his right foot to slowly push the door the rest of the way open. With his gaze darting from left to right, he did a quick sweep of what he assumed was Sophie's bedroom.

He checked behind the door before moving into her private space. It smelled like her, all strawberries and cream, and Sophie.

But there was another scent filling his nostrils...gunpowder.

"Sophie?" He said her name but got no response.

At first glance he didn't see anyone, but the room was fairly large.

The cool, evening breeze brushed past him, drawing his attention to a small sitting area to his right. A set of sheer curtains framed a large picture window there, one that had recently been broken.

Keeping an eye out for any possible threat, Jason quickly made his way over to the window. With his heart in his throat, he looked through the jagged opening to the dark space below.

Lying in the grass was a cushioned chair matching the one he was currently standing next to. Had the intruder followed the piece of furniture, or had he simply made it look as though he had?

A low groan had Jason spinning on his heels. With his gun pointed out in front of him, he took slow, purposeful steps toward the other side of the room.

He cleared the master bathroom with ease, and then headed for the walk-in closet. The door was slightly ajar, and the light was off, so Jason approached the area with the same caution he'd used earlier.

Controlling his breathing, he pushed the door the rest of the way and slid his free hand up the wall in search of the light switch. When his fingers brushed it, he flipped the switch, instantly illuminating the large space.

The air in his lungs froze from the sight before him.

Sophie was lying on the floor in a growing pool of blood. And she wasn't moving.

"Sophia!"

Jason holstered his weapon and ran to her. His knees hit the plush carpet beside her still form, and he held his breath as he put two fingers to the side of her exposed neck.

There!

Her pulse felt weak, but it was there. With a quick assessment, he found the source of the blood—a bullet wound to her upper left arm.

Jesus, she's been shot!

"Sophie?" He wrapped a hand around her wound and held on tight. "Baby, can you hear me?"

A soft moan was her only response.

"Sophia!" Jason sharpened his tone. "I need you to open your eyes."

Her eyelashes began to flutter. After a long, agonizing moment, her brown eyes were staring back up into his.

"Jason?"

He wanted to cry with relief.

Thank you, God. "Just stay still, sweetheart."

Using his free hand, he yanked out his phone and dialed the only Dallas detective he trusted to take on this case. The seconds it took for Eric West to pick up felt like hours.

"West."

"It's me."

"Ryker? What's up, man?"

"There's been a shooting. I need your best people on it, including you."

There was a pause and then, "You do know that's not how this sort of thing works, right? You can't just call and demand—"

"I need you on this one, Eric," Jason cut the fucker off. "Consider it a personal favor."

"So...you'll owe me one? Damn." The other man chuckled. "That's a mighty tempting offer."

Jason ground his teeth together. "Eric."

"Wait." The detective's tone changed. "You're serious?"

"As a fucking heart attack."

Some papers shuffled around in the background. "What's the address?"

Rattling off the address to Sophie's house, Jason quickly added, "And send a bus."

"Who's the victim?"

"Sophia Ruiz."

"Dr. Ruiz from your hospital?"

"Yes. Gunshot wound to the upper left arm. Looks like a graze, but it's bleeding like a bitch and she lost consciousness."

"Hang on." Eric put him on hold, presumably to notify dispatch. Within seconds he was back. "I've got units and an ambulance on the way. You get the shooter?"

"Negative." Jason shook his head in disgust.

But I'll find the bastard.

"I'm leaving the station, now," the other man informed him in a rush. "I'll be there in less than twenty."

He ended the call and tossed his phone onto the carpet beside him. The agent in him wanted to process the scene and figure out who the hell had done this to her.

The man in him refused to leave her side for even a second.

"Soph? Baby, I need you to stay with me."

"I'm okay." She nodded weakly. "Just a…scratch."

A scratch that had already caused her to lose too much damn blood.

"That's right." Jason brushed some hair from her face. "You're going to be just fine."

She had to be. He wouldn't accept anything less.

Chapter 5

"You were really lucky, you know that?"

Sophie looked up at Olivia as she checked the dressing covering her wound. "I know." She nodded. "I still can't believe someone shot at me."

"He didn't just shoot *at* you, Soph," Jason growled. Pushing off the wall he'd been leaning against, he looked like a man on the edge as he stalked toward her. "If that bullet had been a few centimeters to the left, it would've torn straight through your brachial artery. I know you know what that means."

Sophie knew *exactly* what that meant. If her artery would've been hit, she would've bled out on her closet floor before he had the chance to find her.

"But it didn't," she reminded him. "And I'm fine."

Okay, so maybe *fine* was a bit of a stretch. When the gun had gone off, the blow from the bullet striking her had knocked her off balance.

She'd hit her head on the edge of her dresser, which was positioned in the middle of the closet, so in addition to a gunshot wound, she also had a mild concussion.

Refusing to leave her side, Jason had hovered over her from the time she'd regained consciousness until Olivia threatened to kick him out of the room if he didn't give her space to work.

The man had growled at Liv—literally *growled*—but then did as he was told and moved to the corner of the room.

He'd stood there the entire time Sophie's arm was being cleaned and stitched, and also during the battery of tests he'd demanded she receive.

With his strong arms crossed in front of him, Jason looked like an angry bear as he stared back at her.

"Don't do that." Jason got into her space. With his hands on his hips, he stared down at her with more emotion than she'd ever seen.

"What?"

"Don't sit there and act like someone didn't just try to fucking *kill* you tonight."

"That's just it," she spoke softly. "I'm not so sure they did."

Olivia frowned. "What do you mean?"

Sophie started to explain when there was a knock on the door. Like the overprotective man he was, Jason went to the door to see who it was.

Stepping aside, he allowed Eric and Riley West to enter the room.

The two Special Crimes detectives had arrived at her house just as she was being loaded into the back of the ambulance. At Jason's request, the husband-and-wife duo had immediately taken over the scene, promising to come to the hospital for her statement later.

Guess it's later.

Eric was the twin brother to Derek, R.I.S.C.'s Alpha Team technology guru. Sophie had met the detective on several occasions, as well as his new wife.

They were both nice, and from what she'd learned over the past couple of years, they were also two of the city's best detectives.

"Hey, Olivia." Riley gave the other woman a smile before turning her attention onto Sophie. "Dr. Ruiz. I'm glad to see you're okay."

"Thanks." Sophie gave her a small smile. "And I'm here as a patient, so please...call me Sophie."

From his spot beside her, Jason grumbled, "She's not fucking okay, Riley. She's been shot and has a concussion."

"A *mild* concussion," Sophie emphasized, lifting her wounded arm. "And it was just a graze."

With a low grunt, Jason crossed his arms at his chest again, the sleeves of his white button-up tightening over his defined biceps.

Damn, he has nice arms.

Giving herself a mental slap on the head, Sophie refocused on the situation at hand.

Eyeing Jason carefully, Eric slid his attention back to her. "We found two bullet holes in your closet. One on the west wall, and another in your dresser. Sounds like you were damn lucky."

Another low grunt escaped Jason's throat, but he didn't say more.

After sharing a look with her husband, Riley said, "Why don't you walk us through what happened tonight, Sophie."

Ignoring the throbbing in her arm and incessant headache that didn't seem to want to quit, Sophie did her best to relay what had happened inside her home two hours earlier.

"Jason and I went to dinner, and—"

"Wait, what?" Olivia's hazel eyes grew wide. "You two went out to dinner? As in...together?"

"Not really the time, Liv," she shut her friend down quickly.

With a look that said she'd spill the details later, Sophie continued on.

"After you and I...said our goodnights"—she slid her gaze to Jason's, praying the others couldn't see the blush crawling up her neck—"I went upstairs to get ready for bed." A shiver raced down her spine as she absentmindedly shook her head. "I didn't even know anyone was there, at first."

"It's okay, Sophie." Riley's tone was soft and comforting. "Just take your time."

You're fine. You can do this.

"I removed my earrings and my watch, and placed them in my jewelry armoire," she went on. "Then I went into the closet to grab my pajamas, and...that's when I saw him."

She didn't tell them that she probably would've noticed the intruder sooner had she not been distracted by the toe-curling kiss Jason had given her minutes before.

The memory had her eyes rising to meet his. Hidden beneath his short beard, a muscle in Jason's strong jaw twitched.

Was he thinking of their kiss, too? She couldn't tell.

Clearing his throat, Eric asked, "Then what?"

"Then...we fought."

"You *fought?*" Jason and Olivia spoke in unison, both looking back at her as if she'd lost her damn mind.

Going hand-to-hand with a burglar wasn't exactly her ideal option, either. But she hadn't really had much choice.

"He was coming out of the closet when I walked in," she told them. "We bumped into each other and I screamed. When I saw the gun in his hand, I...I don't know. I guess my fight or flight instincts kicked in, because the next thing I knew, I was going for the gun."

Jason muttered a low curse under his breath as he rubbed a hand over his jaw.

"Is that when you were shot?" Olivia asked quietly.

Sophie shook her head. "The man and I...we were fighting for control of the weapon. It went off once and the bullet went wide. The guy pushed me into the dresser. He started to run away, so I went after him."

"You did what?" Jason shot her an angry scowl.

"I wasn't thinking, okay?" She blinked away a sudden onslaught of tears. "My body just sort of reacted."

"It's okay, Sophie," Eric stepped in. "Just tell us what happened next."

"I think I may have screamed again, but I'm not a hundred percent sure. I just remember the sound of a second gunshot and then white-hot pain in my arm. The next thing I knew, I was waking up and Jason was there...and the guy who'd broken into my house was gone."

Riley blew out a slow breath. "Lucky for you, Ryker showed up when he did."

"Yeah." Sophie looked over at him, his tight expression undecipherable. "I'm very lucky."

The room went silent, and Olivia's gaze bounced back and forth between Sophie and Jason. "I'm going to go see about getting you a private room for the night."

"I'm not staying." Sophie peeled her focus away from Jason to look at her friend.

Olivia's eyes softened. "Soph, you lost consciousness."

"The wound on my arm isn't serious and the concussion is mild. I know what to look for as far as warning signs."

"I figured you'd say that, but I still had to try." With a sigh, the other woman walked over to the plastic chair in the corner. Grabbing a set of scrubs from the seat, she set them at the foot of the bed. "Your dress had blood on it," Olivia explained. "I thought you might want to change into these. I'll find Dr. Nichols and let him know he needs to get the discharge paperwork ready. I'm assuming you won't be allowed to stay at your house. My shift doesn't end for another hour, but you're welcome to come home with me."

Crap. With everything going on, Sophie hadn't even thought about where she'd go after she left the hospital. Even if it wasn't an active crime scene, her bedroom window had been smashed wide open by the jerk who'd broken into her home.

"She's staying with me."

Sophie's eyes shot to his. From the expressions on the others' faces, they were just as shocked by his statement as she was.

"I appreciate the offer, Jason, but that's not necessary."

"It sure as hell *is* necessary," he bit back. "You heard what Liv said. The doctor wants to keep you in the hospital for the night. So either you stay here, or you come home with me. This isn't up for discussion."

Uh...yeah. It actually was.

Straightening her spine, Sophie told the overbearing man, "I get that you're used to ordering everyone around, but I'm perfectly capable of making my own decisions. Especially when they concern my safety."

"Your safety is the reason I want you at my place."

Because he cared for her, or because he felt some misplaced responsibility for what happened?

Does it matter?

"I'll give you two a moment to discuss your plans for discharge." Olivia excused herself and left the room.

"I think we have all we need for now," Riley spoke up next. "If either of you think of anything else, give us a call."

"Thanks, Riley." Sophie looked over at Eric. "You, too, Eric."

With a nod, the two detectives started to leave, but then Eric turned back around. "I almost forgot to ask…did the perp say anything to you before you blacked out?"

"Not that I recall, no."

"Okay. Again, if you remember anything, even the smallest detail, let us know. And when you're feeling up to it, we'll need you to go to your house and see if anything's missing. The sooner, the better. Just don't go alone."

"You don't have to worry about that," Jason assured him.

The two men shared a look before Eric and Riley left for good. And for the first time since coming to the hospital, Sophie and Jason were completely alone.

She knew she should probably say something but wasn't sure what that something should be.

The last few hours had been such a rollercoaster of emotions. A myriad of events ranging from amazing to terrifying. All leaving her uncertain and confused.

He'd been so caring and compassionate at her house and then while he held her hand in the ambulance on the way here. But then, after being forced to let her go, Jason had grown quiet and surly.

And now, he was demanding she go home with him.

His intentions were pure. Of that, she was certain. The problem wasn't him…it was her.

She had a hard enough time remembering to *breathe* when she was in the same room as him. How the heck was she supposed to survive spending an entire night with the mouthwatering man?

Especially after that kiss.

Not really what you should be worried about right now.

The voice in her head was right. He was only offering to take her to his home so he could take care of her. Not because he wanted to seduce her.

But that kiss he'd given her earlier had made Sophie want to throw all her inhibitions to the wind and jump his damn bones.

Hellooo....Break-in. Gunshot wound. Concussion. Remember?

Damn, she was having a hard time keeping herself in line. Maybe she hit her head harder than she thought.

Or maybe the man standing in front of her was making it impossible to concentrate on anything else.

You need to say something. Anything to break this awkward as heck silence.

"Thank you." Sophie said the first thing that came to mind. "I know it isn't enough after all you've done for me, but I don't really know what else to say."

"You don't have to say anything, baby." His dark eyes remained on hers as he took a step closer.

Baby?

Her heartrate increased and her mouth went dry.

Jason's swallow was audible. "You can trust me, Sophia. I'd never take advantage of you or any other woman. Especially not when you're in a vulnerable situation like this. I need you to know that."

"I do trust you, Jason," she responded instantly. She felt like shit for making him think otherwise.

Appearing confused, he said, "If you trust me, why don't you want to stay with me?"

"My hesitation to accept your offer isn't about mistrusting you."

His dark brows turned inward. "Then what's the problem?"

Just tell him.

"I don't think..." Sophie licked her suddenly dry lips. Drawing in a deep breath, she exhaled slowly before admitting, "I don't think I trust *myself*."

Their gazes remained locked, the sound of her own heartbeat filling her ears. When he didn't respond right away, she thought the admission had been a huge mistake.

But then...

"I didn't think I was going to get to you in time." He lifted his hand, resting his callused palm against her cheek. "I heard you scream, and then I heard the gunshots, and I...I couldn't move fast enough."

"But you *did* get to me." She leaned into his touch. "I'm still here because of you."

Jason started to move closer, his intentions to kiss her clear as day. But then his phone began to ring, cutting the moment short.

Lowering his hand, he pulled the phone from his pocket. With a muttered curse, he said, "It's work. I have to take this."

A strong sense of déjà vu struck, the scene similar to the one on the plane weeks before.

This is what life with a Homeland Agent would be like. Stolen moments between phone calls and classified meetings.

The thought wasn't a criticism or complaint. Just an observation.

As an emergency room doctor, Sophie understood better than most what it was like to have a crazy, unpredictable schedule.

Jason's job was important. *Really* important. No way would she make him feel guilty for doing it.

"Go." She smiled up at him. "It's not like I'm going anywhere without you."

Surprise flickered behind his wary gaze a fraction of a second before his lips curved. "I'll be right outside."

Watching him go, Sophie was still shocked by the awful turn their wonderful evening had taken. Deciding to make use of her time, she slid off the bed and began changing into the set of scrubs Olivia had been kind enough to procure.

Careful not to bust open her stitches, she'd just gotten the top pulled down when Olivia knocked before peaking her head in and asking if she was decent.

"I'm good. You can come in."

"Here's your paperwork. You know what it says, of course. But I still have to give it to you."

"Thanks." Sophie took the papers and set them on the mattress beside her. Turning back to her friend, she stared back at the other woman and sighed. "Ok, let's have it. Go ahead and ask."

Olivia frowned. "Ask what?"

"Come on, Liv. I know you're dying to ask about my dinner with Jason."

"You've been through a lot, Soph. I don't need to know—"

"We kissed," she blurted the news.

Olivia's eyes grew as big as saucers. "You *kissed*? When? How was it? Start from the beginning and don't leave anything out."

Sophie chuckled. "After you left the cafeteria, he asked me to dinner. He said he had some follow-up questions, but apparently that was just an excuse."

"I *knew* he liked you." Olivia's grin spread from ear to ear. "Go on, and hurry...before he comes back."

Sophie didn't get into the whole discussion about Colton Moore and her theory as to why those men in Djibouti had been after him. She simply shared that they'd had a nice time and she'd gotten to know him a little bit better over a delicious meal.

"Yeah, yeah." Olivia motioned with her hand. "Get to the part where he kissed you."

"I'm getting there." Sophie grinned. "After dinner, Jason drove me home and walked me to my door."

"And? How was the kiss?" Olivia looked like a kid at Christmas while she waited to hear all the juicy details.

"It was"—incredible, earth-shattering, amazing—"the best kiss I've ever had."

"Seriously?"

Sophie nodded. "Seriously."

"And now you're going to go spend the night with him."

"Only because he feels obligated to protect me."

That and she couldn't go back to her own place. Not that she really wanted to. Which, in and of itself, brought on a whole separate set of emotions.

Sophie loved her house, and she'd worked damn hard to make it into a home she felt comfortable in. A place where she'd always felt safe.

Not anymore.

She'd heard about how victims of home invasions sometimes moved because they couldn't handle the constant reminder of what happened. Just thinking about walking back into her closet sent a barrage of nerves racing through her system.

"Hey." Olivia grabbed her hand. "You okay?"

"Yeah." Sophie shook her anxiety away. "I'm fine."

"You know people who keep repeating that they're fine are usually anything but. I know this because, for a while there, I was the queen of being 'fine'".

"Really, Liv." She squeezed the other woman's hand. "I'm a little shaken up, but I'm good."

With a watchful eye, her friend let her hand drop. "You know I was just teasing you about Ryker. If you don't feel comfortable staying at his place, just say the word and I'll have Jake come pick you up."

"It's late. There's no reason for Jake to wake Lily up to come all this way just to get me."

"He wouldn't mind, and Lily always loves seeing her Aunt Sophie."

Aunt Sophie. That's what Olivia and Jake always called her when their cute-as-a-button daughter was around.

"It makes more sense for me to stay with Jason. He's already here, and I know I'll be safe with him."

"You sure about that?" Olivia teased.

Sophie laughed. "I'm sure. He was a perfect gentleman tonight. Besides, my head and arm are killing me, and even if they weren't, I'm too tired to even think about sex."

At least she hoped she was. Otherwise, it was going to be a long damn night.

"Wow."

Her brow furrowed. "Wow, what?"

"You and Ryker."

"She and Ryker, what?" Jason chose that exact moment to re-enter the room. He was staring back at her with a raised brow, clearly expecting a response to his question.

Shit. Please tell me he didn't hear everything we said.

Olivia, God bless her, quickly came to her rescue. "Uh…I was just telling Sophie how lucky you both were. I mean, if that guy hadn't taken off, who knows what would've happened."

Sophie watched Jason closely, but she couldn't tell whether or not he believed the woman's story.

With a tip of his chin, he grabbed his suit jacket from the chair where he'd left it and slipped it over his broad shoulders. "You ready?"

"Yeah."

Grabbing the paperwork from the bed, Sophie started to walk to the door. She stopped cold when she realized her feet were, well, *cold*.

"My shoes." Her head swung back and forth between the other two. "I wasn't wearing any when that man—"

Before she could finish the sentence, Jason was there. Bending at the waist, he wrapped one arm around her back and the other behind her knees.

Sophie let out a tiny squeal when he lifted her up as if she weighed nothing.

"What are you doing?" She instinctively wrapped her arms around his neck to keep from falling.

"Solving a problem."

From behind her, Sophie heard Olivia mutter, "That's one way to do it."

"Jason, really." She did her best to sound stern. "I can walk."

"I know you can."

"Then why don't you put me—"

"Please," he whispered softly, his brown eyes holding onto hers. "Let me do this."

The request had Sophie's heart skipping inside her chest. She gave him a single nod, and without another word, the big, alpha male turned and carried her from the room.

Chapter 6

"Wow." Sophie moved further into the entryway of his home. "This is incredible."

"You sound impressed." Which, for some strange reason, was a huge relief.

Jason knew he had a nice home. He was a single guy who made a shit ton of money running the covert unit for Homeland.

With no one to share it with, and barely any life outside of work, he could afford to make his home his sanctuary. But this was the first time he'd had someone here whose opinion mattered, so the uncertainty he'd felt when she first walked in was unsettling, to say the least.

Relax, man. She likes it.

She also looked really, *really* good in it. As if it had been built just for her.

The modern, open-concept structure was filled with smooth, clean lines and contrasting hues. Everything in it had been designed with intent and purpose.

The dark gray tile floor, white walls, and stained wood trim complimented each other perfectly, and he'd carried the theme throughout the entire house.

His large, sunken living room was centered around the floor-to-ceiling stone fireplace, and the enormous picture window on the opposite wall faced his patio and pool in the back.

It was after midnight, but the solar lights that were strategically placed lit the area up enough to still see.

Turning to face him, Sophie's face lit up the entire room. "I *am* impressed. Of course, I'm sure every woman you bring here is equally so."

"I don't bring women here." The confession, ripped from somewhere deep inside, had Sophie blinking.

"Ever?"

He moved his head back and forth slowly. "You're the first."

"Wow." She seemed genuinely surprised. "So, at the end of your dates, you...what? Go back to their place?"

"I don't date."

This left her blinking even harder. "Why not?"

He didn't want to lie. Not to her. But he wasn't ready to tell her the truth, either.

"My job is very demanding," he went with his default excuse. "It doesn't leave me with a lot of free time. When I am able to get away from work, I'm here, enjoying the peace and quiet."

"I can appreciate that." She spun in a slow circle, taking everything in. "So what do you do to unwind?"

"Read or watch old movies."

The built-in bookshelf to her right caught her eye. She went to it and started scanning the titles there.

He knew what she was seeing. *Charles Dickens, Harper Lee, Emily Brontë...*

As she perused his selection of hardback novels, Sophie asked, "What kind of movies do you like to watch?"

"The black and white kind, mainly." When she smiled, his brows turned slightly inward. "What?"

"You're a romantic."

Jason felt his frown deepen. "I literally just told you I don't date."

"And?" She sauntered back toward him. "I haven't been on an actual date in months. Doesn't mean I don't enjoy stories with heroes and movies with happy endings."

Her admission stirred something within him. But instead of digging deeper into why she hadn't had a date in so long, Jason shrugged a shoulder, his mouth curling into a cocky grin.

"Sorry to burst your bubble, sweetheart. But I'm probably the least romantic male you'll ever meet."

"I don't accept that."

He barked out a laugh, the echoing sound unfamiliar in his typically silent home. "You don't *accept* that?"

"Nope." Sophie jutted her chin playfully.

"Do tell."

"You have a home meant to be admired by others. The living room furniture is positioned around the fireplace in a way that would allow for conversation and entertaining. You have fresh flowers on your dining room table, and your bookshelves are filled with the classics. And while some aren't exactly what most would consider to be romance novels, many do include elements of romance mixed into their complex plots."

Intrigued by the way this amazing woman's mind worked, Jason couldn't help but grin. "Go on."

"Well, everyone knows the black and white movies are the best kind to watch, especially for those who take joy in those final scenes where the leading man kisses the leading woman, and the viewer knows they're going to end up living happily ever after. And that pool out back?" She turned toward the window. "There are two lounge chairs around the fire pit. Not just one. That suggests you want someone else to occupy it, even if you don't actually ever extend an invitation for someone to come over."

He walked over to her, his dress shoes clicking lightly across the tile as he moved. "Are you finished?"

She pretended to think before nodding. "I think so."

"You have a very astute eye." He stopped a few inches in front of her. "Now I'm the one who's impressed."

"What's the real reason you don't date?" she pushed the subject.

Jason wanted to tell her the truth, but he couldn't bring himself to say the words. He couldn't tell her he avoided relationships because being with him had cost the woman he'd loved her life.

It cost me fucking everything.

"I told you, I don't have time for relationships."

"Because of your job."

"That's right."

Sophie stared up at him, her eyes saying she didn't buy it. Not that he should be surprised. The woman was too damn sharp for her own good.

Still, she didn't push the subject. Instead, she started to ask about a painting on his wall, but a large yawn kept her from it.

"It's late," he pointed out the obvious. "You should really get some rest."

Sophie nodded. "I'm really tired, all of a sudden."

"It's the crash. Your body's way of telling you it's had enough."

"Listen to you, sounding like the doctor." Another yawn struck and she covered her mouth with her hand until it was over.

"Come on. I'll show you to your room."

Leading the way, he and Sophie went up his wooden staircase to the second floor. When they reached the only room there, he opened the double-doors and stepped aside, allowing her to enter the room before him.

Her soft gasp reached his ears as she took in the intimate space. "Jason." She turned to him. "This is *your* room."

"I'm aware." He grinned.

"What I meant is, I don't need to take your bed. I can sleep on the couch or..."

"You're not sleeping on the fucking couch, Soph," he bit out more harshly than he intended. Pulling in a calming breath, he added, "I have a futon in my office. I'll take it, and you can sleep in here."

"That makes no sense."

"It does, actually. I have some work I need to do, so I'll probably be up for a few more hours. The spare room is right next to my office, so its best if you sleep in here, where you won't be disturbed."

"But—"

"No buts, sweetheart. Now, make yourself at home. The bathroom is in through there"—he pointed to a set of doors to his left. "There are clean towels in the tall cabinet by the sink, and a spare toothbrush in one of the drawers."

Speaking of drawers...

He went over to his dresser and pulled out one of his t-shirts. Shoving the drawer shut, he went back to her and held it out for her.

"You can wear this to sleep in tonight." He handed her the garment. "If you're feeling up to it, we can go to your place in the morning to pack up some of your things and bring them here."

Her pretty eyes rounded. "Exactly how long are you planning on having me stay here?"

"Until I know you're safe."

"It was a break-in, Jason. I seriously doubt the guy's planning on coming back."

"We can't know that for sure." Especially given the incident in Djibouti. "Eric and Riley are doing all they can to find the intruder, and when they took you back for a CT, I put a call into McQueen. He's going to get someone to fix your window, and his team is also installing a top-of-the-line security system so we can keep an eye on things. In the meantime, you can stay here. With me."

Both of Sophie's brows rose high. "Guess you've thought of everything."

He *had* thought of everything. Including putting out feelers to see if there was any way this was connected to Djibouti.

The likelihood was slim, but after seeing Sophie lying on that floor—bleeding and unconscious—he wasn't taking any chances.

Never with her.

"I'd argue with you, but I know you're right." Her soft voice pulled him back to the present. "I can't stay at my place, and I've been meaning to get an alarm system put in. I just kept putting it off. So, if you're sure I won't be imposing..."

"Not an imposition, sweetheart."

She offered him a tiny smile. "In that case, thank you."

Unable to stop himself, Jason let his knuckles trace the delicate skin of her cheek. "I already told you, you don't have to thank me."

She moved inward, bringing her body closer to his. "I do have one question."

"What's that?"

"Why are you doing all of this?"

Jason nearly jerked back from her words, but then realized it was a very valid question.

Of course, she doesn't know.

How could she? He'd spent the last four years intentionally keeping a wide distance between them.

Though it was sometimes hard, given their interconnected jobs, he'd forced himself to avoid any and all situations that might put him in a position where they would be alone.

Where he'd be tempted to give in to the urges he felt every time he laid eyes on her. Where he might forget why he'd vowed never to get that close to anyone ever again.

If you let people in, you risk living with the pain of losing them.

Another woman's face flashed before him, but he pushed it away. Like he always did when memories of her—and what they'd shared—haunted him.

So, no. Jason hadn't let *anyone* in. Not since that fateful day ten years ago. But he'd also never been tempted...until Sophie.

The woman was standing three feet from his bed. Her mouth less than two inches from his. And Jason found it nearly impossible to hold everything he was feeling inside.

Running his knuckles down the length of her cheek, he said, "I have to keep you safe."

"But why?" She reached for his hand. She held onto it with her own as her eyes searched his for the answer. "You've risked your life twice for me, now. We've known each other for years, yet I barely know anything about you."

I know everything about you.

Well, almost everything. There was more he needed to know. More he *craved* to learn.

Like what she would look like falling over the edge in his arms.

"We've had one sort-of date," Sophie continued with her list.

"Your point?"

"My point is, you're going through all this trouble for me, and I just...I don't understand why."

"Honestly?" Jason huffed out a breath. "I can't explain it." Lifting their joined hands to his mouth, he pressed his lips to her knuckles. "All I know is the second I saw your name on that AMOVA list, I knew *I* had to be the one to come for you. And tonight, when I heard you scream my name, God himself couldn't have kept me from running to you."

Her lips parted at his shocking admission, her small intake of air telling.

"Jason?"

"It's late, sweetheart. You need to get to sleep, and unfortunately, I need to work. We can pick this back up later, yeah?"

"Promise?"

He couldn't help but grin. "I promise."

Framing her face, he leaned forward and pressed his lips to hers. "Are you hurting? I can get one of the pills the doctor prescribed you if you need one."

"I'm okay, for now."

"Come find me if it gets worse?" he asked softly. "I hate the idea of you being in pain."

"I will. Now, go." She gave him a gentle shove. "Do whatever it is you have to do."

"I'll be downstairs if you need me."

With another quick kiss to her forehead, Jason forced himself to turn and walk away. He didn't even glance back before shutting the bedroom door behind him for fear he'd never leave.

Before heading to his office, Jason made a detour to his kitchen. Fixing himself two fingers of his favorite whiskey, he carried the short glass through the hallway on the other side of the main floor, where his office was located.

As he made his way to his desk, he did everything in his power not to think of the woman upstairs. Or the fact that she would be sleeping in his bed.

Jesus, walking away from her had been hard. A certain area of his body was *still* hard.

A chronic issue he suffered from any time she was around.

He'd seen the heat in her eyes when he'd kissed her just now. Could see the heady beating of the pulse point in her neck.

It would be so easy. All he'd have to do is go back upstairs, kiss her the way he had before all hell broke loose, take her to his bed, and...

She's injured, dickhead. Get your mind where it belongs.

Shifting in his seat, he adjusted himself as best he could, opened his computer, and started scanning through emails. Not exactly the mandatory work he'd led Sophie to believe, but he didn't trust himself to stay in that room a second longer and not do more than just kiss her.

For the next hour, Jason responded to the messages in his inbox, all the while trying desperately not to picture Sophie hurt and bleeding. Fucking *shot*.

Just like...

Nope. He was not going there. He couldn't go there.

Forcing the memory and fear away, Jason reminded himself over and over again that she was upstairs right now...and that she was okay.

When the emails had been taken care of, he moved his focus to the file next to him. The one containing the latest intel on Colton Moore, who was still nowhere to be found.

Jason read over the reports again, hoping something might stand out to him. That he might find an answer as to where the man was or who his possible abductors were.

They'd received no communication from him or anyone else claiming responsibility for his disappearance. There'd been no ransom demands or political propaganda with Moore at the forefront.

It was the one thing that continued to nag at Jason's insides.

Usually, when a journalist was taken hostage—especially an American one—the group behind the kidnapping can't wait to show off what they'd done.

Groups like Al Qaeda and the Islamic State—formerly known as ISIS—were notorious for their so-called political statements and public executions in the name of a God they couldn't possibly worship.

So far, there hadn't been a single form of communication with or about Colton Moore. A fact that settled in Jason's gut like a pot full of lead.

With sleep finally calling his name, he closed the folder and stood. Glancing at the aforementioned futon, he decided instead to sleep on the couch.

In the living room—which would allow him to hear Sophie better if she needed him—he removed his gun and holster and laid it on the coffee table. Slipping off his jacket, he flung it over the back of his leather recliner before toeing off his shoes.

With sluggish movements, he proceeded to remove his socks, pants, and shirt, placing them on the chair with the jacket. Wearing nothing but his boxer briefs, Jason pulled the gray throw blanket from the back of the couch and flopped his tired body onto the cushions.

As far as sleeping went, his couch wasn't the most comfortable piece of furniture he owned, but he'd sleep on the damn floor if it meant Sophie was comfortable and safe.

Though he was both mentally and physically drained, sleep still didn't come easy. Jason's mind replayed that terrifying scene from Sophie's house, over and over again like some sort of nightmare marathon.

Then, when he did manage to make his way past the horrifying loop, he found himself the newest contestant in the what-if game from hell.

What if he hadn't heard her scream?

What if that bullet had hit her chest and not her arm?

What if he'd found her dead instead of unconscious?

What if I lost her?

Sometime during the vicious cycle, sleep finally, *finally* pulled him under. His dreams were a mixture of his worst fears and his strongest desires.

Both versions starring the woman who was quickly worming her way into his hardened heart.

It was in the midst of a particularly good dream when Jason woke to the sound of Sophie screaming his name. On reflex, he shot up from the couch, grabbed his gun, and sprinted toward the stairs.

Heart racing, he burst through his bedroom door. With his gun held out in front of him, he was ready to take on whatever threat dared to loom over his woman.

Head on a swivel, he did a visual sweep of the room. Within seconds he realized the only intruder was the one Sophie was seeing in her dreams.

Lying in the middle of his king size bed, she tossed and turned. Kicking and pushing away a man who wasn't really there.

Jason had no idea which form of evil her mind had created—Abdul Qasim or the man who'd attacked her in her own home. All he did know was that she was trapped in a nightmare and the sight was breaking his fucking heart.

"Please don't," she begged the person trying to hurt her in her mind. "Jason!"

He couldn't do it. He couldn't stand here and watch her relive the trauma she'd endured. Not when she was calling for him to save her.

Fuck it.

Setting the weapon on his nightstand, Jason rested a knee on his mattress and reached for her. Careful not to touch the bandaged area on her arm, he gave her shoulder a gentle shake.

"Sophie?"

She moaned and turned her head, but her eyes remained closed.

"Wake up, Soph. You're dreaming."

"Please, don't." Her plea was a low mumble.

"Come on, baby. You need to wake up."

With another shake, Jason was about to try raising his voice when Sophie's eyes flew open as she gasped. Jerking back, she scrambled to get away from what she believed to be a dangerous threat.

He held both hands up to show her he meant her no harm. "You're okay," he assured her. "It's just me."

"Jason?" Her disoriented gaze moved around the room. She looked down at the gun and then back to him. "What happened? Is something wrong?"

"You were dreaming." He released a breath. "From the way you were screaming, I'm guessing it wasn't a good one."

Clearly mortified, Sophie said, "I *screamed?*"

"You, uh..." He rubbed the muscles at the back of his neck. "You called out for me."

"I did?" Though the room was only lit by the moonlight in the distance, her apology was clear in her chestnut eyes. "I'm sorry I woke you."

"Nothing to apologize for, sweetheart."

A few seconds passed between them, the fear and confusion in her gaze becoming heated as it lowered with the dips and ridges of his bare chest and abs.

Until that moment, he'd forgotten he wasn't wearing anything more than his boxer briefs.

Although, from the look on her face, Sophie didn't exactly seem to mind.

"What, uh...what time is it?" She brushed some hair from her face and brought her gaping stare back up to his.

Her voice was raspy with sleep, the sound reminding him of passion and sex.

Reaching out, he turned the clock located on the bedside table, next to where his gun was. "Three thirty-five."

With a moan that made him almost swallow his own tongue, she rubbed the sleep from her eyes and looked back at him. "Did you even get any sleep?"

"A little." He dipped his head toward her bandage. "How's the arm?"

"It's throbbing a little."

"And your head?"

Sophie reached back, wincing when her fingers hit the sensitive spot. "Sore, but manageable."

"I'll be right back."

Not giving her a chance to argue, Jason went back downstairs and got the pain meds. Grabbing a bottled water from his refrigerator, he carried them both up to his room where Sophie was still sitting up in the same spot where he'd left her.

"Here." He popped open the prescription and tapped two pills out into his palm. "Take these."

"I don't know that I need—"

"You're hurting." He handed her the water. "And you need to rest. These can help with both of those things." When she hesitated, he lifted a brow and asked, "What would you tell your patients?"

"You play dirty." Sophie swallowed the pills and downed a big gulp of water. Setting the bottle onto the nightstand she licked her damp lips.

I'd sure as hell like to play dirty with you, Doc.

"Thank you."

He gave himself a mental head slap. "You're welcome."

Settling her head back down onto the pillow, she pulled the covers up to her chin and sighed.

"Better?"

"Better." She nodded, her hair making a swishing sound as it brushed back and forth on his pillow.

More than anything, Jason wanted to go to her. His body itched to lay down next to her and hold her in his arms. To give her the comfort he knew she needed in order to find a peaceful sleep.

For years, he'd avoided relationships in order to keep from feeling the pain. Standing here now, seeing this amazing woman in his bed, he realized he'd do anything to take her pain and make it his own.

Picking up his gun, he turned to leave when he heard Sophie's soft voice beckon him.

"Jason?"

He faced her once more. "Yeah?"

"Would you mind staying? Just until I fall asleep?"

She's scared.

This strong, fiercely independent woman who'd traveled halfway around the world to help others was scared to be alone.

Jason was filled with a sudden jolt of urgency to find the son of a bitch who'd caused that fear and make them wish they'd never been born.

"Never mind." Sophie blurted, her voice bringing him back from his murderous thoughts. "Forget I said anythi—"

"I'll stay."

Without a word, Jason set his gun back onto the small table and climbed into his bed. Adjusting the covers so they were over them both, he wrapped his arm around her waist and pulled her back to his front.

He nearly groaned when he felt her smooth, bare legs brushing up against his. Wondering what the hell he'd been thinking, he prayed she couldn't feel the growing erection that had a mind all of its own.

Jason closed his eyes and breathed in her sweet scent. His body molded around hers perfectly, as if they were tailor-made for one another.

"This okay?" His voice rumbled as he worked to slow his racing heart.

"Yeah."

Her hand slid over his, which was resting snuggly against her flat belly. She already sounded more relaxed, the tension in her muscles easing as he held her close.

"Thank you," she whispered again so softly he barely heard it.

Jason threaded his fingers with hers as he dropped a kiss on the back of her head. "Go to sleep, sweetheart. You're safe here."

Within minutes Sophie was sound asleep. But for Jason, sleep didn't come until much, *much* later.

As he lay in the dark, with Sophie sleeping like an angel in his arms, his thoughts took him into the past.

Of a love—and a life—that was previously lost. Both stolen from him in the blink of an eye.

As it often happened late at night, when no one was around, memories of the pain and heartache Jason had suffered all those years ago assaulted him.

The agony from that day was as fresh as if it had just happened, but he pushed it back, like he always did. Refusing to let it take over.

Sometime later, as the dark of night slowly began to break into the dawn, those heartbreaking thoughts morphed to something different.

Someone different.

And as he held on tight, giving Sophie the comfort and safety he knew she needed, Jason began to wonder if maybe...just maybe...he was ready to try again.

Chapter 7

Sophie woke engulfed in a blanket of muscle and heat. When she opened her eyes, she felt confused and disoriented, and it took her a full five seconds to realize where she was...and who she was with.

Holy crap! I slept with Jason!

It all came back to her in a single, jolting rush.

The nightmare.

The screaming.

Jason waking her up in nothing but his boxers.

Him sliding into bed and pulling me into his arms.

She'd slept in Jason Ryker's bed. The man was *still* in his bed. And his strong, toned arm was draped across her midsection, pinning her to the mattress.

Sophie turned her head and found his sleepy gaze staring back at her.

"Morning." His deep voice resonated within her.

Her breath stuttered inside her chest. "Good morning."

She wasn't sure what to do next. Should she try to get up? Stay where she was?

He was probably waiting for her to make the first move, so he didn't come off as an insensitive jerk.

Turning to his side, Jason reached up, his fingers feathering across her forehead to move a few strands of hair from her eyes. "You're so beautiful."

Oh, my.

In an attempt to keep things light, she teased, "I think your eyesight is diminished first thing in the morning. You might want to see a doctor about that."

Humor had his face lifting into a real, honest to goodness smile. The first one she'd seen him wear in...forever.

"You've got jokes, Doc. And even before caffeine. That's impressive."

With a chuckle, Sophie started to shift onto her side to face him directly, but winced when the wound on her arm rubbed against the mattress.

"Careful." Jason frowned. "How badly does it hurt? Do you need another pain pill?"

She wasn't a fan of narcotic meds. They'd always knocked her for a loop, and Sophie hated not being in control of her faculties.

"Maybe just some ibuprofen." She yawned a huge, embarrassingly large yawn. "And Coffee. Definitely coffee."

"I'll go make us some."

"You don't have to wait on me hand and foot while I'm here, you know."

Cupping her face, his thumb brushed back and forth against her cheek as he told her, "I like taking care of you."

Okay, who is this man and what has he done with the hard-nosed Homeland agent I know?

Not that she was complaining. Sophie could totally get used to this softer, sweeter version.

"I should check in with the hospital." She sat up and leaned against the headboard. "Let Dr. Nichols know I'm still alive and kicking."

A thought struck just then. One that had Sophie cursing under her breath.

"What's wrong?"

"My phone. My purse, my keys...they're all at my house."

Jason pointed to the nightstand behind her. "You can use my phone. As for your other things, we need to go by your house today, anyway. Tell you what, why don't you make your phone call and get dressed, and we'll head over there after breakfast?"

"Breakfast?" Sophie's brows arched high. "You cook?"

"I can hold my own in the kitchen."

"Good to know."

Throwing off the covers, she swung her legs over the edge of the mattress and stood. It took her half a second to remember she was dressed in her panties and Jason's gray t-shirt.

Thankfully, the hem fell halfway to her knees.

She turned to ask him if she could use his shower, but the question was caught in her throat when she saw the expression on his face.

It was all primal heat and male arousal. And it was all because of her.

Clearing her throat, Sophie choked out, "Do you mind if I use your shower?"

His eyes darkened even more than they already were. "Make yourself at home."

"Thanks," she whispered.

Then, because she didn't really know what else to say, Sophie spun on the balls of her feet and headed for the bathroom.

After taking full advantage of Jason's enormous, custom shower with all the bells and whistles, she dried off and got re-dressed in the scrubs Olivia had procured for her. quickly using the new toothbrush Jason had told her about last night, Sophie found a comb and ran its teeth through her thick, damp hair.

Deciding to let it air dry, she put everything back in its place and headed downstairs to the kitchen.

"Something smells amazing." She found Jason standing at the stove. He was wearing a pair of well-worn jeans and a hoodie.

This was a side of him she never knew existed, and though she didn't understand it, the casual, laid-back look did funny things to her insides.

Good grief, Sophie. It's just a hoodie.

Ignoring her inner voice—because hoodie or not, he looked damn fine—she made her way over to the pot full of freshly brewed coffee.

"What are you making over there?" She filled the mug he'd set out for her to just below the rim.

"Ham, egg, and cheese crepes. I also have sauteed mushrooms, fresh spinach, and green onions if you'd like me to add any of those to yours."

"Wow." She found herself saying that a lot around this man. "When you offered breakfast, I pictured something easy, like scrambled eggs and toast."

"Crepes are easy," he commented. "If you know what you're doing."

Walking over to him, she glanced over his shoulder and watched the magic happen. Sophie knew her way around the kitchen, as well. But she was more into baking than cooking.

"You want any of the added fillers, or just the ham, egg, and cheese?"

"Um..." She bit her bottom lip while looking at the selections. "I'll take some spinach and mushrooms, please."

"You got it." He winked.

Leaning her back against the counter near the stove, she took a sip of her steaming beverage. Closing her eyes, she moaned. "I swear, there's nothing better than that first sip of coffee in the morning."

Sophie nearly spilled her coffee when she felt Jason's lips on hers. With a start, she opened her eyes in time to see him pulling back, licking his lips as he moved.

"You're right." His gaze smoldered. "Nothing better."

"Okay, seriously. How is it you're single?"

The question just slipped out. An innocent comment meant to be funny and lighthearted. But the way Jason's expression fell told her it had been anything but.

He returned his focus to their breakfast, flipping one of the crepes in the pan.

Sophie watched as he continued cooking the delicious-looking food in silence. Minutes passed, the uncomfortable quiet filling her stomach with dread.

When she couldn't take it anymore, she told him, "I'm sorry if I offended you. That wasn't my intention."

Scooping two twin crepes onto the plate waiting to the side, Jason turned off the burner and set the spatula back into the empty pan.

With a sigh, he turned to her, his eyes filled with a mixture of sorrow and trepidation.

"I'm the one who needs to apologize. I haven't been completely honest with you about why I don't date. Why I live in this big house alone, and why I've kept my distance where you're concerned."

Though she was dying to know what he'd been keeping from her, Sophie said, "Jason, really. You don't have to—"

"I do, actually." He picked up the plate with their food and motioned toward the table on her left.

Noticing the two place settings already waiting for them, Sophie took her coffee and headed that way. When they were seated, she waited for him to say what he needed to say.

"I was engaged, once." He dropped the bomb quietly and without much emotion. "I was twenty-eight and Shelby was twenty-six. We were college sweethearts."

So, ten years ago.

Sophie watched him closely, several scenarios running through her mind at once.

Had he been left at the alter?

Had he left *her* at the alter?

Had he found her in the back of the church with her dress hiked up and his best man's pants around his ankles?

Rather than guess, she decided to ask. "What happened?"

"Everything was perfect." His broad shoulders shook with a humorless laugh. "I'd been working for Homeland for six months, we'd gotten a really nice apartment in the city, and…" He let his voice trail off for a bit, this next part clearly hard for him to say.

"It's okay, Jason." Sophie spoke softly. "You can tell me."

Pain filled his eyes as he said, "Shelby had just found out she was pregnant. We were ecstatic."

Oh, god. Something about the way he said it…the way he *looked*…said this was about more than just a jilted lover.

Drawing in a deep breath, he let it out slowly before continuing on. "Two months before the wedding, I was assigned my first major case with the agency. A case *I* was in charge of. Since Shelby had taken care of the details of the wedding, I worked day and night to help the team bring down one of the country's top organized crime bosses. A guy who, at the time, was still very much in business."

Sophie's heart sunk. This story was definitely not going to end well. Not at all.

"We got him though." He smirked, though there was disdain shining in his gorgeous eyes. "We got him and his whole crew. And since it was my first big bust, I was able to personally cuff the guy and take him in."

Something happened after. Something bad.

"Three weeks before the wedding, we'd gone to the tux shop for my final fitting. Shelby insisted on going with me. She wanted to make a day of it. First the fitting, then lunch. After that, we were going to shop for things for the baby's room."

Keeping her breathing steady, Sophie waited on pins and needles for him to finish the story.

"We were walking to my car when this blacked-out SUV drove past. I was looking down at my phone, answering a text from my boss when I heard Shelby scream my name." He blinked quickly, his eyes glistening with unshed tears that broke her heart in two. "She pushed me out of the way, putting herself in the bullet's path."

"Oh, Jason."

"She was dead before she hit the ground. In a split second, I lost her and our baby. I lost...everything." He sniffed and lifted his coffee mug to his lips.

Sophie suspected the drink he was taking was a way to help stave off the unwanted emotions. She knew this because she'd used the same trick a time or two.

"It wasn't your fault."

"My fiancée died because she took a bullet meant for me," he bit out sharply. "My baby never even had a chance because some asshole mob wanna-be thought he could impress the imprisoned boss by taking out the man who put him away."

"So that's why you don't date," she surmised from her place across the table. "You're afraid someone will come after you again. And if you allow yourself to become vulnerable by falling in love, then you open yourself up to the pain of losing them."

"I've made a lot of enemies doing my job, Sophie. More than you could count."

"Yet, you're still here."

"But the family I was supposed to have isn't." He shot up out of his chair, nearly tipping it over in the process.

Standing slowly, Sophie followed him into the living room. He stood at the large picture window facing the pool. His back was to her, his arms crossed tightly at his chest.

"What you went through was horrific." She moved closer. Risked putting a hand on his shoulder blade. "I won't insult you by trying to pretend to understand what that was like for you. But when I think of what you do, of the lives you save every single day... Those lives are invaluable, but they shouldn't come at the cost of your own."

Dropping his hands to his sides, Jason turned to her with a hardened expression. "When I lost them that day, I swore I would never put myself in a position to feel that way again. I threw myself into my work, and I've spent the last ten years taking down every goddamn criminal I can get my hands on."

"Your dedication to the citizens of this country is commendable. But don't you want more for yourself?"

"Of course, I do." His brow furrowed. "I wanted it all. Love, marriage...kids. But that ship has already sailed."

"Says who?"

"I'm thirty-eight years old, Soph. Not to mention, I'm already married to my job."

"So am I." She shrugged. "Well, I'm thirty-six, but you know what I mean. My schedule's unpredictable. It's filled with crazy hours, phone calls in the middle of the night. I've gotten called in on weekends...holidays. I understand having to drop everything at a moment's notice. I also know how easy it is to use that as an excuse not to ever really put yourself out there."

Jason's pain morphed into curiosity. "Did you lose someone, too?"

"Not in the way you mean. I've lost opportunities. The potential to build something real. But like you, my experiences with loneliness were of my own doing."

"What do you mean?"

"I grew up in a household where marriage meant pain and fighting. Where, one minute my dad was telling my mom how much he loved her. How he'd never be able to live without her. And in the next, I'd see him slamming his fist into the side of her face."

"Soph—"

"Don't." She put a hand up to stop him. "I'm not asking for sympathy, and frankly, I don't need it. I've made something of myself, despite my toxic childhood. And because I grew up like that, I know what I want and refuse to settle for anything less."

Jason opened his mouth. He started to say something but stopped himself. Licking his lips, he tried again. "What is it you want?"

"The same things you want. Love, marriage...hopefully it's not too late for kids." She sighed. "But I want all of that with someone who understands and accepts how important my job is to me. That and the fact that I'm not going to give it up for them or anyone else until and unless *I* choose to."

"That seems fair."

"Relationships should be about two people growing together. Supporting each other in their goals and lifting each other up when times get rough. That's what I want."

"And that's what you deserve."

"It's what we both deserve." She put a hand to his defined chest. "That's what I'm trying to say. Obviously, I'm not suggesting we run off to Vegas and get married. I mean, you haven't even taken me on a real date yet."

A low chuckled burst from his smiling lips. "You aren't going to let that one go, are you?"

"Nope. Not until it happens."

"Oh, it'll happen." He put his hands on her hips and pulled her body flush with his. "I just need to look into your break-in a little further, first. Make sure it actually was a random act of violence and not something more."

"You're not going to let *that* one go, are you?" She grinned.

"I can't." He ran a hand over the hair on the back of her head. "I can't risk missing something. Not with you."

Part of her wanted to tell him she wasn't his late fiancée. That he didn't have to live in fear that something like what happened to Shelby would happen to her, too.

But then she remembered she'd almost been shot and killed in Djibouti. And she *had* been shot last night, in her very own home.

So she kept those thoughts to herself and decided to just live in the moment. With him.

Rising onto her tiptoes, Sophie pretended not to notice the impressive bulge nudging against her lower belly as she nibbled his bottom lip.

"The food's getting cold," she whispered teasingly.

He feathered his mouth against hers. "We could always…heat it up later."

With a devilish grin, Sophie let her lips slide across his and said, "I think that's the best idea I've heard all day."

Chapter 8

Jason took Sophie's hand and led her back upstairs, to his bedroom. His heart pounded against his ribs so hard, he was almost afraid the damn thing was going to burst free.

He didn't know what had compelled him to tell her about Shelby and the baby. He never talked about them with anyone.

But this was Sophie. She brought things out in him he'd buried ten years ago, alongside his fiancée and child.

It was crazy and made absolutely no sense. Sure, they'd known each other for years, but they didn't *know* each other. Not like this.

That didn't matter.

Things were moving fast between them. He knew that. Yet at the same time, it felt as if it had taken forever for them to get here.

Now that they finally *were* here, Jason's hesitation and worry were suddenly all but gone.

Maybe telling her about his loss all those years ago had somehow set him free. Maybe by giving Sophie that piece of himself, he was finally able to fight for something other than justice for victims and vengeance against the bad guys.

He could finally reach out and take what he'd wanted all along. What he knew in his jaded heart was his.

I want her. Heart and soul, I want her.

Making his way to the bed, Jason stopped several inches away and turned to her. "Are you sure about this? If not, we can—"

She put a finger to his lips, cutting off his words. "I'm sure."

Thank Christ.

Relief flooded him as he let the tip of his tongue slide along the digit. Sophie's breasts rose with her sharp intake of air, her pupils expanding with the same desperate heat filling every inch of his body.

Wrapping his fingers around her tiny wrist, Jason pressed his lips against her palm. The inside of her wrist. The sensitive skin just below the inside of her elbow.

Pulling her close, he wrapped her arm around his waist as he reached up and cupped her cheek. "I've wanted you for so long," he admitted in the quiet of his room. "It's been killing me not to be able to hold you like this."

"I've wanted you, too," she smiled up at him. "From the day we met, I've dreamed of being with you like this."

Well, hell.

"I should've said something sooner." His eyebrows pulled inward. "We've wasted so much time."

"We're here now." She moved into his touch. "You're here, and I'm not going anywhere."

"Sophie..."

"Make love to me, Jason. Please."

Jason slid his hand under her hair and leaned over her. His lips found hers in a barely controlled kiss.

She wasn't tall, a full foot shorter than him. He'd have to take his time and go slow. Use a gentle touch, and not give in to the raging caveman begging to be set free.

The last thing he ever wanted to do was hurt her. Not his Sophie. And he was finally realizing...finally accepting...that she was his.

Or at least she was about to be.

Sophie was warm and kind with a beautiful smile and a mouth that could make him laugh. And she was smart. Much smarter than him, apparently.

He'd spent a decade denying himself the chance to be happy, and in one soul-bearing conversation, she'd made him see that he deserved more.

He didn't deserve *her*. Jason knew that to the very depths of his soul. Sophia Ruiz was much too good for a man like him.

But Jason also knew he was a selfish asshole. He'd loved this woman from a distance for far too long. And like she'd just said, she was here...and she wanted him.

Make love to me Jason. Please.

No matter what he did in life, he would never be good enough for her. That wasn't something he had the power to change.

But he was tired of running from life. From *love*. And that was something he *could* change. Starting now.

Everything Jason had always wanted was right there. All he had to do was reach out and take it.

Which was exactly what he intended to do.

Sophie opened her mouth to him. Her tongue met his in an explosion of sweetness and pleasure. Jason swallowed her moan as he took the kiss deeper.

She moved her hands up, grabbing hold of his shoulders to keep herself steady. With his hand on her lower back, he pressed their bodies even closer together.

His aching erection pressed against her belly. Her firm breasts molded against his chest. It was everything and not enough, all at the same time.

With his mouth still on hers, Jason guided them onto the mattress. He lay on his back, pulling her on top as her thighs reflexively straddled his.

Sophie's soft waves fell over their faces, like a curtain shutting out the rest of the world. In an unexpected move, she sat up. Tearing her lips from his, she carefully removed her scrub top and bra.

The bandage covering the wound on her left arm filled him with rage. But the rest of her...

"Jesus," Jason choked out the sentiment when he caught sight of her bare breasts for the very first time.

They were perfectly proportioned to her petite body. Her nipples were the color of a dusky rose, exactly as he'd pictured them in his mind so many times before.

They were tight and reaching for him from the center of her firm globes, and he couldn't *not* touch them a second longer.

Jason lifted his hands, filling them with her offering. Sophie closed her eyes and let her head fall back, the sight alone damn near causing him to come in his pants right then.

"Perfect." He sat up, taking one of the taut nubs between his lips before teasing it with his teeth. "You're so fucking perfect."

"Jason!"

He gave the other breast the same attention. His tongue playfully teasing her nipple as he had the one before.

Her body instantly responded, her pelvis grinding against his as he pleasured her with his mouth. Jason wasn't even sure she realized she was doing it, and on reflex, he lifted his hips in response.

His steely cock pressed against her hot core and he released a low moan. Even through the thick denim of his jeans, Jason could feel her body's welcoming heat.

He knew she was ready for more, and he was more than ready to oblige.

With his arms wrapped tightly around her to keep her from falling, he stood and spun them around. Laying her on her back gently, Jason began leaving a trail of wet kisses down the center of her toned midsection.

He stopped when he reached the waistband of her pants.

"These are in my way." He toyed with the tied drawstring.

"Yeah?" She gave him a sensual smirk. With her hair splayed out all around her, she asked him, "What are you planning to do about that?"

"Oh, I plan to do a lot." He pulled the drawstring loose and proceeded to untie it completely. "So, so many things."

Dipping his fingers into the sides of the waistband, he began pulling them and her silken panties down as she lifted her hips off the mattress.

Though he wanted to rip the damn things off, pull out his greedy cock, and drive himself into her for days, Jason forced himself to move slowly. Patiently.

And it damn near killed him to do it.

Tossing the clothing to the side, Jason stood at the edge of the bed and stared. The air in his lungs froze, her beautiful, gorgeous body literally taking his breath away.

"Perfect," he growled. Yep, he actually fucking *growled*.

But that's what happened when an animal was about to mark its prey. No, not his prey.

My mate.

She was completely bare, the glistening lips of her sex calling for him. His mouth watered just thinking about the fact that he was seconds away from getting his first taste.

His dick pressed against his zipper to the point of pain. He'd probably have a permanent mark there, but that was fine with him. It would serve as a reminder that he was just as much hers as she was his.

Bringing his gaze back to hers, he kept their eyes locked as he pulled his hoodie up and over his head. Sophie's brown eyes darkened with desire, much like they had when they'd first woken up this morning.

Jason had wanted to take her then, but he'd held back for fear it was too much, too soon. Looking at her now, though...the way her eyes and body were begging for his touch...there was no doubt in his mind that she was ready.

Releasing the button on his jeans, he carefully lowered his zipper before shoving his jeans and boxer briefs down his thighs and off his bare feet.

A low, satisfying moan escaped the back of Sophie's throat, and when he noticed she was hungrily staring at his protruding cock, he stood stock still, letting her take her fill.

"Like what you see?"

"I'd like to touch it even more."

His hard length bobbed in response, the eager bastard more than willing to let her do whatever the hell she wanted. But first...

I have to taste her.

Stepping up to the mattress so his legs touched the edge, Jason placed his hands on her knees and eased her legs apart. With his breath catching, he felt a tingling of anticipation as he slowly slid his palms along her upper legs to the juncture between her thighs.

"Jason," she panted his name again.

God, he *loved* hearing her say his name like that.

"Don't worry, baby," he rumbled. "I'll take good care of you."

It had been a long damn time since he'd been with a woman he wanted to make love to. Sex? Sure. He had that now and again.

With women who didn't know who he was or what he did. And they never wanted to know. Just like he had no desire to delve into their lives.

For a decade, now, Jason's sex life consisted of the occasional hookup with someone who knew and appreciated the situation as well as he did. Casual, no-strings pleasure with a mutual agreement to walk away after.

He was always safe. Always. And he made sure the women he was with walked away satisfied.

But that life had gotten old a long time ago. His encounters had become fewer and fewer, and when he met Sophie, they all but stopped completely.

Because of her, but also because of him. It wasn't the kind of man he wanted to be. And if he needed release, he'd turned to taking care of it himself.

For a long time, now, when he took matters into his own hands…there was only one woman Jason pictured in his mind. One woman who filled every sexual fantasy he'd ever had.

The same woman waiting anxiously for him to make the move that would change everything between them.

You've wasted enough time, Ryker. Now's your chance to give her the pleasure you've only dreamed about before.

He leaned down and brought his mouth to her core. Her sweet, musky taste exploded on his tongue as he traced her slit before diving into heaven.

He'd never tasted anything like it.

Jason continued to drink his fill. Beneath his mouth, Sophie writhed and moaned as he licked and laved and sucked. But it wasn't enough.

Never enough.

While he continued to consume the gift she was offering, he reached between her legs and slid a finger into her molten heat. Jason moaned against her sex as he felt her inner muscles grip onto him like a vise.

Can't wait to get inside her.

Sophie cried out when he began pumping his hand while simultaneously flicking her swollen bundle of nerves with his tongue. He added a second finger, stretching her tight body to prepare it for his.

He knew she wasn't a virgin, but it was clear from the way she felt around his hand that it had been a while for her, too. Not wanting to risk hurting her, Jason knew exactly what he needed to do to help get her ready.

He thrust his fingers in and out of her body with more speed and force than before. His tongue swirled expertly around her clit, pressing down just enough he wouldn't cause her pain.

Sophie's hands filled with his hair, the sensation just this side of painful. He didn't care.

From the way she moved and the sounds she was making, Jason knew she wasn't just enjoying what he was doing. She was about to erupt.

Confirming this, she panted, "Oh god, Jason! I'm close!"

Knowing he was bringing her the ultimate pleasure spurred Jason on. He sped up even more. Moved in and out of her wet body at a pace he knew would soon bring with it an incredible detonation.

And when he placed his lips around her clit and sucked, she erupted in his arms.

"Ah!" Sophie cried out as she threw her head back.

Her hips flew off the mattress, her entire body shaking from the force of her orgasm.

Jason drew out every ounce of pleasure he could give before sliding his hand free and making his way up the length of her body.

"Christ, that was beautiful." He kissed her collarbone, her pulse point, her chin.

"I think I may have actually died for a second," she teased, her rough voice sounding sated.

I did that for her.

Wanting to pound his chest like the fucking caveman he was, Jason refrained and instead chose to bring his lips to hers. "You ready for more?"

"Yes, please." She lifted her lower half, letting her drenched sex rub along his painfully hard dick.

Jason moaned, nearly slamming himself balls deep right then. But a thought struck out of nowhere, and...

"Shit." He froze. "Condom."

"Do you have one?"

He shook his head. "It's been a really long time, and I just never bought anymore."

"How long?" She asked curiously.

"Nearly a year."

It was a pathetic admission, he knew. He was a healthy, single, full-grown man. And now she probably thought there was something seriously wrong with him, because—

"It's been over a year for me," she told him softly.

"Really?"

Sophie grinned. "High expectations, remember?"

And she'd chosen to go to bed with him.

His heart raced inside his chest. "I'm clean. We get tested every six months. But if you want to stop, I completely understand."

His painfully swollen cock would hate him forever, but he would never try to coerce a woman into sleeping with him. Ever.

"I'm clean, too. And since I work for Homeland, as well, I also get tested twice a year."

Did that mean...

"I've never had sex without a condom." He needed her to know. "Except for Shelby, and she..."

"It's okay, Jason." Sophie pressed a palm to his rough cheek. "I trust you."

The heart he thought was destroyed so long ago became filled with a love he never dreamed was possible.

Too emotional to speak just then, Jason reached between their bodies and lined himself up to her entrance. With his eyes glued to the woman who may very well have saved his soul, he pushed his hips forward, sliding into her blissful heat in one, powerful thrust.

Their moans of pleasure sounded in unison. Sophie's lips parted, her eyes closing shut as he seated himself so fully, it was impossible to determine where he ended, and she began.

Holy fuck, she feels amazing.

Still, he had to ask, "Are you okay?"

It would kill him if he was causing her pain.

"I'm good." She nodded, her eyes finding his once more. "More than good."

The smile spreading over her face was all the incentive he needed.

With his weight resting on his forearms to keep from crushing her, Jason slowly pulled back before pushing forward again.

His eyes damn near rolled back into his head from the intense physical pleasure this woman had created inside him.

She gave and he took. Together, they used their joined bodies to remind themselves what life was really all about.

Though their jobs were very different, both Sophie and Jason spent their days fighting to save people's lives. But as he continued making love to her, he realized she was right about everything.

He did deserve to live again. To experience love and pleasure, and all the other things he'd thought were lost to him forever.

And he wanted that for Sophie, too. He wanted to see her happy. Smiling and laughing...and he wanted to be the man by her side making her do those things and more.

I want to be the one to bring her to ecstasy. Over and over, again. Only me.

As far as Jason was concerned, she was his now. His to love. His to protect.

Mine.

The rhythm in which their bodies moved increased. His thrusts became stronger. More powerful.

And when he felt Sophie begin to tremble, ready to fall over the edge again, Jason was right there with her.

"Ah, fuck," he growled. "Ah, yeah, baby. Just...like...that!"

He ground out her name as a mind-blowing climax shot its way through his system. Sophie cried out again, her body melting all around his for the second time.

By the time Jason returned to his euphoric state of bliss, he realized he was lying fully on top of her.

"Shit. Sorry." He withdrew from her sensitive entrance, immediately missing the void her body had filled.

"That was...wow." Sophie huffed out a satisfied breath.

With his eyes closed, Jason laid on his back and grinned. "Wow, is the perfect way to describe what that was."

"We should've done that a long time ago."

His grin turned into a full-blown chuckle. "Agreed." He turned onto his side. "Except, in a way, I think our timing is perfect."

"How so?" She faced him, too.

"I don't know. I guess I believe everything happens for a reason. At least, I used to believe that."

"I think so, too. And I think"—she scooted across the bed toward him—"if we'd done this sooner, it probably would've been a one-off. A way to release stress or blow off steam. So, I'm glad this happened now. Like this."

"So there'll be a second time?" He knew the answer but felt compelled to ask.

"And a third." She gave him a soft kiss. "And a fourth." Sophie rubbed her cheek along the soft stubble of his beard.

"You're shooting mighty low there, Doc."

"Yeah?"

Jason dipped his chin. "I'm thinking triple digits. At least."

"Triple?" Sophie's eyes widened with a smirk. "That could take a while, Agent Ryker. Are you sure you're up for that?"

"I'm sure." He kissed the tip of her nose before bringing his lips to hers. "I'm in this for as long as you'll have me."

"Careful what you offer there, mister. I might have to keep you around just to see how long you can last."

"That sounds like a challenge."

Sophie smiled wide. "Maybe it is."

"Well." Jason pulled her into his arms and held her close. "I've always loved a good challenge."

Chapter 9

Sophie walked into her home. Except it didn't really feel like a home, anymore.

It was the place she'd been attacked. Violated by an unknown man who'd broken in and gone through her things.

"You okay?" Jason asked from his place beside her.

He'd asked her that same thing when he'd been inside her less than two hours ago.

She still couldn't believe they'd had sex. No, not just sex. They'd made love.

This strong, stoic, handsome man had shown her pleasure in ways she'd never imagined she could feel.

When he'd told her about his fiancée and unborn child, her heart had shattered for him. As a doctor, she'd delivered news of a loved one's death numerous times. It was the hardest part of her job.

But to have your loved one die in your arms, that was a pain Sophie prayed she never had to feel.

"Soph?"

She blinked, realizing she hadn't responded to his question. "I'm good." She nodded. "Just ready to get this over with."

"Come on." He placed his hand on her lower back and guided her up the stairs. "We'll get you packed and then you can walk through each room and see if you notice anything out of place."

There was an officer stationed on the road in front of the house. Jason had spoken with him when they'd first arrived.

She hadn't listened too closely to the conversation but heard enough to realize he was there at Jason's request.

The man sure has some pull in this city.

For the next few minutes, Sophie went about packing some clothes, shoes, and toiletries into her larger suitcase. As she did, she looked around her room to see what, if anything, had been moved or altered.

The only place that appeared disturbed was her closet. It was a total mess.

Something she hadn't noticed during the break-in, because she'd been too busy fighting for her life and then getting knocked out.

Clothes were strewn about. Her suitcases had all been opened and tossed to the side.

Some boxes containing a few photos and keepsakes had been taken off the shelf running along the north wall and opened. Their contents scattered all over the top of her dresser and floor.

The thing that stood out to Sophie the most was the blood stain that had soaked into her light beige carpet.

I could've died right there, in that very spot.

"I wish like hell I'd been able to catch the bastard," Jason bit out through clenched teeth.

Sophie blinked and glanced up to find him staring at the dark crimson stain, too.

"Me, too." She put a hand on his arm. "But I'm also glad you scared him off, so he didn't have the chance to shoot me again."

Heavy emotion swirled behind his eyes, and she realized everything between them had changed.

A week ago, he was a man she secretly pined over. An hour ago they were making love and talking like there was a future between them.

And now, the man who'd seemed more machine than human most days was staring back at her in a way that said he cared far more than she'd ever believed possible.

"We should check the other rooms," she suggested. Mainly to tear him away from his somber thoughts. "See if any of them look like this."

Sophie turned to leave, only then noticing the picture window that had been shattered was already fixed. "I didn't even...who...how in the world did that get fixed so quickly?"

"I told you, I asked Jake and his team to take care of it."

"Yeah, but"—she glanced at her watch—"it's not even noon."

"They're the best at what they do for a reason, sweetheart." He leaned down and kissed her temple. "Jake sent a text while you were still sleeping. Said this had been completed and they'd be out this afternoon to install the security system."

"Boy, they sure work fast." Another thought had her feeling a sliver of disappointment. "Wait, if that's fixed and the system is being put into place today, then why am I packing my things?"

"Because we still don't know who attacked you or why."

"Right, but Jason...that could take months. And that's assuming the police even find the guy."

He simply shrugged "Then it takes months."

"I can't move in with you for that long."

"Why not?"

"Why..." She chuckled. "Because we've barely even begun to date."

"This is about me keeping you safe." He turned to face her directly. "You said you trusted me."

"I do."

He nodded. "You also said you wanted to be with me."

"Again, I do, but—"

"What better way to get to know someone than by living with them?"

Sophie blinked. "You're serious."

"I am." He put his hands on her hips and sighed. "Look, I get that I'm going from zero to a hundred right now, and I honestly don't mean to. So let's back up. For now, you'll stay with me for your safety and protection. Period."

"And after?"

"After the cops catch the son of a bitch, we can revisit the discussion about us and see where we want to go from there. That sound like something you can get on board with?"

"Yeah." She smiled.

Sophie thought he was finished, but then Jason's voice got quieter. Softer. And he shocked the hell out of her when he said, "For the record, we both agreed earlier that we've wasted a lot of time not going for what we wanted. Lord knows, I have. And I'm not sure how you did it, sweetheart..." He licked his lips before continuing on. "But you've changed something in me. Something that, even if I wanted to, I don't think I could ever change back."

"I feel different when I'm with you, too," she confessed.

"I'd say that's a good start." He smiled. "Now, come on. Let's get through the rest of the house, and then we can call Eric and relay our findings."

Less than an hour later, they'd walked through every room in the house. Sophie had looked over every piece of furniture. Every picture frame. Every book on every shelf.

As far as she could tell, nothing else in her home had been disturbed except her closet.

"The asshole was looking for something specific." Jason stood in her living room with his hands on his narrow hips.

His jeans and hoodie had been replaced with a pair of navy-blue dress pants and one of what she suspected to be many of his white button-up shirts. He'd left the jacket at home, though.

Something Sophie found herself inwardly smiling about.

Maybe he is becoming more relaxed.

"Why do you think the man was searching for something in particular?" she asked, curious.

"Because he hit the one place in your house you'd most likely keep stuff hidden. Your suitcases, the boxes...all places you might conceal something you don't want anyone to see.

"Like what? I have nothing to hide from anyone. I don't even keep cash in the house." That's what her bank was for.

"Is there a safe anywhere? A place you might have put important documents or heirlooms?"

"I don't have any heirlooms, and all my important documents, like my mortgage and insurance paperwork, are in a safety-deposit box at my bank."

Jason ran a hand over his beard and absentmindedly glanced around the room they were in. "And there's nothing of major value here? Jewelry, artwork...nothing?"

"My jewelry collection is minimal because I'm always working. And the artwork you see mostly came from too many nights of online shopping. Not from a fancy gallery."

She watched his wheels turning, wishing she could read his mind. Luckily, she didn't have to.

"Maybe you're right." He grabbed the back of his neck and started rubbing the muscles there. "Maybe this was random. You have one of the nicest homes on your block. Maybe our guy was hoping to get lucky and find a wad of cash stashed away in your closet."

That's what I've been trying to tell you.

Sophie couldn't fault him, though. One thing she was learning quickly was that Ryker was nothing if not thorough.

And protective.

"So, what now?"

"Now, we call West."

She sat on her couch and waited while Jason made the call. After explaining that nothing was disturbed, other than the things in her closet, he then told the detective about their thoughts and theories.

From what she could make out, Eric agreed. While they were still keeping the case open and active, most likely the intruder was long gone and was smart enough not to come back.

To be on the safe side, however, Jason had convinced her to still stay at his place for the next few days. That would give Jake and the rest of R.I.S.C. plenty of time to get the new security system installed and test it out, and make sure the coast was clear as far as the almost-burglar was concerned.

Not that it took a lot to convince her. Like him, something had shifted inside her over the past twenty-four hours. She prayed it wasn't just some sort of adrenaline-induced love affair.

She'd seen those before, and like that one nineties movie starring Keanu Reeves and Sandra Bullock claimed, those kinds of relationships rarely lasted.

Putting her bags in the trunk of his car, Jason shut the lid and walked to the driver's door. Sliding behind the wheel, he turned to her and asked, "You hungry?"

It had been a few hours since they'd finally gotten around to eating the crepes. While delicious—even re-heated—they hadn't been terribly filling.

"I could eat."

"Anything particular sound good to you?"

"Well, let's see..." She thought a moment. "We had French for breakfast. Want to do Mexican for lunch?"

"A woman after my own heart." Jason winked and started the car. "I know this perfect little authentic place up north. Family owned, great food. If you like Mexican, you're gonna love—"

His phone began to ring, the peal of a sound filling the car's interior.

"Damn. That's work." With an apologetic look, he dug his phone from his pocket and answered, "Ryker."

His expression changed from relaxed to high alert in the span of a single heartbeat. Whatever he'd just been told was not good.

"Are you sure?" His tone seemed to drop an octave. Jason listened to the person on the other end of the line and then, "Thanks for letting me know. I'm headed there, now."

When he ended the call, he shot off a text to an unknown recipient. His phone dinged almost immediately with a response.

Bringing his unreadable expression back to her, he said, "I have to go to the office. It's urgent."

"Oh." She hid her disappointment, understanding

"I'm not sure how long it'll take. I just checked with Jake and he and Olivia are both home. Would it be okay if I took you there until I'm finished?"

"Their ranch is pretty far out of your way, isn't it? Besides, you said Jake was coming here later, anyway. Why don't I—"

"There's no way in hell I'm leaving you alone in that house."

Placing her hand over his, Sophie said, "I know you're still worried about that man coming back to hurt me. But I promise I'll stay inside and at the first sign of trouble—"

"Not happening, Soph. I'm sorry. I just can't...I can't risk it."

She thought back to their earlier conversation. To what happened to the woman he'd loved and lost.

He needs this. Do this for him.

"Okay." She nodded. "Take me to Jake's. But you'd better let him know I expect some Mexican food when I get there."

This time Sophie was the one to wink and smirk. Jason gave her a ghost of a smile that didn't come close to reaching his eyes.

Something was wrong. *Very* wrong, from the look on his face.

His job was filled with classified intel. Chances were, even if Jason wanted to tell her about whatever was going, he couldn't. So she wasn't going to put him in the awkward position of having to deny her request.

Several minutes later, they were entering the secured gate at the entrance to Jake and Olivia's private drive.

Sophie had been to the beautiful ranch before when Olivia had invited her to a girls' night while the guys were away on some secretive op. The log home was gorgeous, the scenery around it, breathtaking.

A large barn sat down a hill to the right of the house. Behind Olivia's home were fields of grassy hills that seemed to stretch for miles.

It was truly one of the most amazing pieces of property Sophie had ever seen.

Jason pulled around the circle drive to the start of the sidewalk and put the car in park. "I'll walk you up."

Sophie climbed out of the vehicle and the two started for the expansive porch. Jason had been relatively quiet on the drive here, and she hated he had to deal with whatever was waiting for him Dallas's Homeland office.

Olivia and Jake met them on the porch.

"Hey, Soph!" Olivia smiled wide. "How are you feeling?"

"Good, actually. Arm's a little sore, but good."

Other parts were sore, too, but in the very best of ways. Of course, she wasn't about to share that with her friend. Not when the woman's husband and Jason were standing right there, too.

"Sophie." Jake gave her a gentle hug. "I was sorry to hear about what happened. You sure you're all right?"

"I'm fine. Really. Just a string of bad luck, I guess."

Olivia and Jake each huffed out a laugh, but Jason was still stuck in Agent mode. Understanding the importance of focusing on one's job, she didn't fault him for this.

"Like I said in my text, I don't know how long this is going to last."

"Take your time." Jake gave Jason a nod. "I've already talked to Trevor. He's going to be on-site to oversee the security installation at Sophie's house in case Derek and the others need any added support."

"Thanks, man." Jason shook Jake's hand. "I appreciate it."

"No thanks needed."

"I'll keep you posted." Jason turned to her. "I'll get back as soon as I can."

"Stop worrying about me. Go do your thing."

For a second, she thought he might kiss her. But since their budding relationship was barely beginning to sprout, she understood why he didn't want to put on a show for their audience.

"You've got your phone?" He glanced down at her purse.

"Phone...and shoes." Sophie lifted a foot and wiggled it.

Smiling at her joke, he dipped his chin and said, "I'll call when I'm on my way to get you."

"I'll be here."

Sophie watched as he drove away. In her head, she said a little prayer that things weren't about to turn ugly for the man who'd seemed to only just be finding himself, again.

Chapter 10

Jason sat in his seat at the long, oval table. His eyes remained glued on the images displayed on the large, retractable screen on the wall he was facing.

His stomach turned, but he refused to look away. His team had failed. *He'd* failed.

And that failure was going to break Sophie's heart.

"We're sure it's him?" He glanced at Admiral Newton, the high-ranking military official standing near the screen.

"DNA confirms the remains belong to Colton Moore."

Damn.

Jason rubbed his hand across his beard. The phone call he'd received while he and Sophie had been in his car was from Dax Tanner, the lead man on his covert team.

Dax had told him Moore's body had been discovered in a trench outside Chabelley, a small village a few miles southwest of Djibouti. With news like that, Jason knew this meeting was vital to shore up any unknowns before the intel was leaked to the press.

Shit like this always found its way to the press.

"Anyone claim responsibility?" He asked no one in particular.

"Not yet," Newton answered. "We're still looking into it, but it's only been twelve hours since the body was discovered. In fact, the only reason we were able to get the DNA results back as fast as we did was because of Homeland's involvement in the case. Sure wish the Navy's labs worked as quickly as yours do."

A few chuckles filled the room, but Jason was no longer in the mood to laugh.

He'd laughed with Sophie earlier. While they were lying in bed after making love. In the shower, and then again while they ate their reheated crepes.

He'd laughed more today—with her—than he probably had in over a year. The feeling had been foreign at first, but then it was like welcoming an old friend back home after a long journey.

Right now, however, the only thing Jason felt like doing was finding the sons of bitches responsible for killing an American journalist in cold blood.

"You got any guesses as to who's behind this, Admiral?" Dax asked from his seat across the table.

The man at the front of the room hesitated to answer, and Jason understood why. In their business, assumptions or guesses could ultimately cost someone their life.

However men like him...and the one they were all waiting on to speak...also knew that, more often than not, their gut instincts were spot on.

"Naturally, our first look was at the Yemeni extremists who attacked the city of Djibouti," Newton commented.

"But you don't think it was them." Jason's words were a statement, rather than a question.

The older man shook his head. "It doesn't sit right for several reasons. The biggest one being the dismemberment and subsequent burning of Moore's body."

"Why does that strike you as odd?" Becca Scott, another one of Jason's invaluable operatives spoke up.

"Because it doesn't fit that organization's M.O.," Newton explained. "That particular group is all about doing things for show. They want the attention. They want public acknowledgement. Dumping a body in the middle of the desert, and then purposely destroying that body to avoid the possibility of it being identified is something entirely different."

Asher Bannon, the brainchild of Jason's team asked, "So how *did* Moore's body get identified?" He jutted his chin toward the large screen. "Looks like there was nothing left but charred bones and ash."

"We got lucky. One of Moore's fingers was found in the dirt, away from the rest of the body. Our guess is, it fell when the pieces were being carried to the ditch. Which is good news for us, because it managed to avoid being burned completely, so your labs were able to access enough tissue to obtain the DNA. Their hit came from a national data base. Apparently, Mr. Moore sent in one of those ancestry kits a few years ago, back when they first became popular."

That answered the how. Now they just had to figure out the who and the why.

"I'm assuming we've also looked into the usual groups," Jason sat back in his chair. "IS, Al Qaeda, Taliban?"

"Affirmative, Agent Ryker," Admiral Newton nodded. "As of right now, nothing with any of those have hit."

"But I'm guessing you have a theory." Jason shot the man a pointed look.

He could tell the other guy's gut was screaming something, and he had a feeling it wasn't good news.

Newton glanced around the room before blowing out a slow breath. "If I were a betting man, which for the record, I'm not, I'd say we need to look into the Syrian government."

"Syria?" Several voices came together at the same time.

"The man you killed"—Newton looked directly at Jason—"was Abdul Qasim, correct?"

Jason sat up a little straighter. "Correct."

"As I'm sure you know, Qasim led the raids in Djibouti the day you and McQueen's team went in. He's also believed to be responsible for several others in the months prior. His group, the Alhukkam, or The All Mighty, took control over Port Sudan early this year. Shortly after, they made some sort of deal with Syria, handing that control over to them."

"That makes no sense." Becca's brows grew close together. "Why would they go through all that trouble just to hand over the very thing they'd fought so hard for?"

"They're terrorists, Miss Scott. Most of what they do doesn't make any sense."

"Except, it does." Jason's wheels began to spin. "If the Yemeni group is somehow working for or with Syria, there may be a hell of a lot more at play here than a bunch of nutjobs looking for attention."

"What are you thinking, Boss?" Dax turned his attention to Jason.

"I'm thinking maybe that's why Moore was killed. Maybe he heard or saw something he wasn't supposed to. Hell, it's possible the raid could've been a cover designed specifically to hide the fact that Moore was their target, all along."

"That's a hell of a leap to make, Ryker." Newton looked directly at him. "You got anything to back it up?"

He thought back to Sophie's account of what had happened in that room before he and Alpha Team got there. "Actually, I might."

Jason recounted Sophie's statement for the others in the room. He told them about how Qasim put a gun to her head and threatened to shoot her if she didn't call Moore to lure him there.

"Son of a bitch." Admiral Newton threw his hands on his hips. "Why am I just now hearing about this?"

"It was need to know, Admiral." Jason remained unaffected by the other man's outburst. "At the time, the theory was that Qasim wanted Moore because of his status as a journalist. Which fit with the way those groups work. Kidnap an American journalist, plaster their face all over the news, then post his execution live for the world to see."

"Except they didn't post it live," Asher pointed out the obvious. "They didn't post it anywhere."

Jason shook his head. "No, they didn't. Which brings us back full circle. We need to figure out why Qasim was looking for Moore. We solve that mystery, we find the bastards who killed him."

"What do we do about the press?" Dax asked

Jason sighed. "We write up a statement for the press. Notify his family *first*, and then release the statement."

Damn it, he did *not* want Sophie hearing about this on some breaking news alert. But even if he texted Jake and asked him to keep her away from the T.V. or radio, she had a phone. Like most Americans with that form of technology, she most likely had hers set to receive notifications whenever a big story like this one broke.

His only hope was to leave now and try to make it to Jake's ranch before the press release went out.

As he gathered his things, another thought hit. One that sent a shot of fear racing down his spine.

If the Syrian government was behind Moore's death, it was possible Sophie and the rest of her volunteer group could be in danger, as well.

And the hits just keep on coming.

With that thought in mind, he stood and started for the door. "I'll be working on this from home," he informed his team and Admiral Newton before exiting the room. "If any of you need me, you know how to contact me."

The immediate and intense need to get to her was damn near overwhelming. Schooling his expression as best he could, Jason said his goodbyes and left.

By the time he got to Jake's, dusk was beginning to settle in. He was five miles from the secluded ranch when his own phone dinged with the dreaded notification.

When Sophie met him at the door, it took all of two seconds to realize she already knew.

"Is it true?" she asked, big wells of tears holding steady in her pretty brown eyes.

"I'm afraid so."

Though she tried holding it in, the tears fell, and her face crumbled. Heart breaking, Jason pulled her into his arms and tucked her head beneath his chin.

"I'm sorry, sweetheart." He kissed the top of her head before resting his cheek there. Rubbing her back, he comforted her the only way he knew how.

"Did they really cut him up and...*burn* him?" Her breathing hitched as she drew in a stuttering breath.

"Look at me." He pulled back enough to frame her face with his hands and look into her eyes. "The details aren't important."

"Don't treat me with kid gloves, Jason. I know I only knew the man for three weeks, but I considered him my friend. This is awful, and my heart breaks for Colton and his family, but I can take it."

Damn, she really was something.

"Yes, they cut him up and burned him," he told her the truth. "Presumably to cover his identity."

"Wait, so if he was burned, then how do you know for sure it's really him?"

"DNA, baby. Trust me, it's him."

"Oh, god." More tears fell, their warmth hitting his hands. "Poor Colton."

"Come on." He put an arm around her shoulder and pulled her close. "Let's go inside for a bit. I need to talk to Jake for a few minutes, and then we can go home."

Leaving Sophie in the living room with Olivia, Jason followed Jake into his home office. Shutting the door behind him, he filled the other man in on what he knew, and what the government's theory was.

Because Jake's company sometimes worked jobs for Homeland and other government agencies, his clearance was almost as high as Jason's. And because he and his team were involved on this particular op, he felt it only fair to read him in on the situation.

"Son of a bitch." Jake leaned against the front of his desk.

"Tell me about it."

"You really think Alhukkam is a cover for the Syrian government?"

"It's a working theory."

The other man ran a hand over his scruffy jaw. "That's a hell of a theory."

"Unfortunately, it's the only one we've got."

A beat of silence passed between them before Jake spoke up again. "I'm assuming you're going to keep Sophie with you while this whole thing plays out?"

Jason stared back at the other man and tipped his chin. "Damn straight."

If there was even the slightest chance someone involved with Alhukkam—or someone with ties to Syria—could come after her, there was no way in hell he'd let anyone else watch over her.

Several more seconds went by and then, "You finally going to admit you have a thing for our mutual doctor friend?"

"I don't have a thing for Sophie." He kept his voice steady.

"Jesus, man. I saw you two on the porch. Just admit it already—"

"I don't have a thing for her," Jason cut the other man off. "I think...I think I might be falling for her."

A slow smile spread across Jake's face. His crystal blue eyes lit with an *I told you so* look, and the asshole beamed because of it.

"Nah." Jake shook his head slowly. "You're already there."

Shit. Fuck. Shit.

"I think you might be right. Ah, Christ." Jason drew in a deep breath to stave off the sudden nausea rolling around in his stomach.

Stumbling over to one of the chairs positioned in front of Jake's desk, he grabbed hold of its padded back and continued his controlled breathing.

"That's it." Jake patted his shoulder. "In and out. Just like that."

"Fuck off, asshole." Jason shook the man's hand off.

"Oh, come on. I was just trying to help."

"Help, my ass. I bet you've been waiting for this moment. For your chance to gloat and tell me how right you were."

"Actually, I've been waiting for this moment because I knew you were a miserable bastard who needed a good, strong woman to set your ass straight."

"You don't understand."

"No?" Jake sat down in the chair next to him and crossed his arms. Propping an ankle over his thigh, he settled in and said, "Why don't you enlighten me?"

Jason's reflex reaction was to tell him to go fuck himself. But when he opened his mouth, his past came pouring out.

He told Jake about Shelby. About the baby. And he told him the story of how he'd lost them both.

"Damn, Jason." Jake stared back at him with both sympathy and shock. "I'm so sorry, man. I can't even begin to imagine..."

"No." Jason shook his head. "No one can. Not unless you've been there."

Of course, back before they were married, Jake had gone several days believing Olivia was dead. So it was possible the other man did know a little something about what he'd gone through.

"Sorry, man." He stared back at his friend and colleague. "I sometimes forget about all the shit that went down before you and Liv tied the knot."

"S'okay." Jake shrugged it off. "I get what you were saying. And I truly am sorry for what you lost. But damn, man. That was ten years ago. You know better than most how fucking short life is. And I obviously never knew Shelby, but...if she loved your dumbass enough to marry you *and* procreate with your hard-headed genes...I'm sure she'd want you to hold onto Sophie and never let her go."

Closing his eyes, Jason took a deep breath in through his nose before releasing it slowly. He pictured Shelby's smiling face. Her short, brown hair. Her bright blue eyes.

And he knew...

"You're right." He looked back at Jake. "If Shelby were here, she'd be smacking me upside the head and calling me an idiot."

She always did call him on his bullshit. It was one of the reasons he fell in love with her.

Sophie does the same thing.

And she was waiting for him in the other room.

"Thanks, man." Jason pushed himself to his feet.

"You headin' out?"

"Yeah. I want to get Sophie home before it gets too late."

"Listen to you, sounding like a man protecting his woman."

That was exactly what he was. And though he felt it was still too soon to say the words out loud, Jason realized he was also a man in love.

Jason got to the door first but stopped just shy of opening it. Looking back at Jake, he swallowed his pride and said, "I owe you an apology."

A fucking huge one.

"For what?" Jake looked genuinely confused.

"I've been an ass. To you and your team. Especially with the guys from Bravo. For a while there, I got so focused on the bigger picture, I lost sight of the real reason we do what we do."

"It happens, man." Jake took it all in stride. "But I'll be sure to pass it along to both my teams."

"I'd appreciate it if you would."

"See?" Jake slapped him on the back. "That woman's already changing you for the better."

Yes, she most certainly was.

After saying their farewells to Jake and Liv, he and Sophie started the hour-long trip back to the city. Sophie was quiet at first, her head leaning back on her seat as she watched the scenery speed past.

She was hurting, and it tore him up inside that he couldn't take her pain away. No, she hadn't known Colton all that long, but for someone like Sophie, that wouldn't matter.

She had a big heart. He'd witnessed this time and time again at the hospital. With her patients. Her staff.

Everyone she came into contact with was better off because of it. Especially him.

Jason reached over and took her hand in his. "Tell me what you need, and I'll find a way to get it for you."

Bringing her eyes to his, she started to tear up again. "This." She held up their joined hands. "This is all I need."

"Then it's yours." He lifted her hand to his lips. "For as long as you need."

Sophie looked back at him and smiled. "Thank you."

With her free hand, she swiped at a tear that had escaped before returning her focus back to the blurred landscape outside.

His chest ached with the need to comfort her. Which was exactly what he planned to do the minute they got home.

Comfort her. Love her. Bring her so much pleasure, she'll at least have a moment's respite from the sadness dimming her normally bright spirit.

Jason thought of all the ways he could accomplish that. The things he could do to her body to make her forget the evils lurking in the world.

He was still mentally planning a night filled with pleasure when a set of bright lights appeared out of nowhere.

Sophie screamed his name just as something slammed into the driver's side of his car. Jason fought to stay in control, but it was already too late.

His tires hit the shoulder's loose gravel before going over the steep embankment. They began to tumble, their world tipping up and over, again and again.

Jason yelled for Sophie. Or at least, he thought he did.

But by the time the car finally came to a stop in the field below, his entire world had gone completely black.

He wasn't yelling for anyone, anymore.

Chapter 11

Sophie moaned, her head throbbing as she peeled her eyes open and looked around. She was dizzy, her mind feeling as though it was floating, somehow.

But then she shifted in her seat, setting off an almost unbearable pain in her right wrist.

She sucked in a sharp breath. Using her left hand, she carefully brought the injured limb to her chest and did a quick assessment.

"Shit. I think my wrist is broken." She blinked a few times to bring the car's interior into focus. "Are you okay?"

Turning, Sophie was instantly filled with fear when she saw Jason slumped over toward her. Blood oozed from a gash in his forehead near his hairline, most likely from smacking against his window, and he wasn't moving.

"Jason!" Adrenaline shot through her veins, kicking her ass in gear.

Doing her best to keep her right arm steady against her chest, Sophie reached down with her left and clicked her seatbelt free.

Ignoring the pain in her head and wrist, she turned her entire body so that it was facing Jason head-on. "Jason?" She reached out and felt for a pulse.

Please be alive. Oh, god. Please let him still be alive.

She found a pulse! It was faint and thready, but it was there.

Phone. I need to get my phone and call for an ambulance.

Looking down, Sophie nearly cried when she realized her purse was no longer in the floorboard near her feet, where she'd placed it. With a quick visual search, she spotted it in the back seat, well out of her reach.

"Damn it."

Jason's phone. Use. Jason's. Phone!

Not wanting to move him for fear he may have a spinal injury, Sophie reached over the console and felt his right pocket.

There!

She could feel the device, but the way he was sitting made it nearly impossible for her to pull it free. Not one to give up easily, she continued grasping and pulling, all the while keeping her right arm as still as she could.

After what seemed like forever, Sophie gave it all she had and finally—blessedly—yanked the phone free.

"Hang on, honey," she told a still-unconscious Jason. "I'm getting us help."

Tears threatened to make an appearance when she saw he had a passcode set up on his phone. But then she saw that it was asking for his thumbprint *or* passcode, so she balanced the phone on the console, grabbed his limp hand, and maneuvered his thumb in order to access it.

Hand shaking, she started to call for an ambulance when his phone began to ring. Sophie jumped at the unexpected noise, but then quickly answered the call when she saw Jake McQueen's name on the screen.

"Jake!"

"Sophie?"

"Oh, thank god. Jason's hurt! Can you send help?"

"What? What do you mean Jason's hurt? What happened?"

"I-I don't know." While Jason drove, her thoughts had been on Colton and his horrifying death. She had no idea how long they'd been on the road. "We were driving home and this car just...it came out of nowhere. Jason's door took a direct hit. He's bleeding from a head wound, and he's unconscious."

Keep it together, Sophie. Jason needs you.

"But he's alive, right? You checked his pulse?"

"Yes." She nodded with a sniffle. "It's weak, but it's there."

"Okay, good. Listen to me. I want you to look around the car. Do you see an emergency button? The kind that calls for help?"

Son of a...why didn't she think of that?

Because you're in shock and scared out of your wits.

Sophie looked on the steering wheel and up near the dome lights. Her heart fell when she didn't find what she was looking for.

"I don't see one." Her voice cracked, but she cleared her throat and kept it together.

She was an emergency room doctor, for crying out loud. She thrived in high-pressure situations.

But this was Jason. The man who'd saved her life...twice. And though it might seem crazy or irrational to some, Sophie realized in that exact moment, he was also the man she was born to love.

"Listen, Soph. I'm already in my truck and on my way to you. I'm going to hang up so you can call 911. I'll be there as fast as I can, okay?"

"Okay. Thanks, Jake."

"I'll see you soon, honey. Hang in there."

Ending the call, Sophie turned to the right when she caught movement from the corner of her eye. She screamed when a man opened her door and began yanking her out of the car.

Agonizing pain shot from her wrist into her shoulder, instantly making her feel as though she were going to pass out.

"Stop!" She tried fighting, but her right arm was useless, and the phone was still in her left hand.

In a split-second decision, Sophie slid Jason's phone into her pocket without the man noticing. Feeling as though she'd just given up her lifeline, she swung her fist around with the hardest left hook she had.

Her knuckles hit her attacker's jaw with precise aim. The man stumbled back, losing his grip on her injured arm.

She started to run. Hard and fast, she headed up the embankment toward the road in hopes a car would drive by and see her.

She made it halfway up the hill when the man slammed into her back, knocking her to the ground.

On reflex, Sophie put both hands out to break her fall. She cried out when her broken wrist rebelled with a sharp, searing pain.

"Ah!" She sucked in a breath. Yanking her hand back, she immediately took the pressure off of her right arm while kicking and screaming as hard and loud as she could.

Please hear me, Jason. Please wake up and shoot this son of a bitch!

Muttering a curse, the man flipped her over onto her back and put a gun against her forehead. The cold metal bit in to her skin, and the memory of Abdul Qasim threating to kill her in Djibouti flashed through her head.

"Goddamnit, Sophie. Stop!"

He knows my name?

Dread twisted in her gut as her terrified mind raced to figure out who this guy was and what the hell was going on.

It was dark, and he had a black hoodie pulled down over his eyes, making it impossible to see his face.

"W-who are you?" Her heart raced and her mind whirled.

Was he looking for money? Drugs? Both?

"I'll ask the questions. Now, where is it?"

That voice.

It was almost...familiar.

"W-where's what?" She trembled with fear.

"Your fucking bag!"

My bag?

"M-my purse is in the back," she blurted. "There's some cash and my credit cards. Take it all! Just take it all and go!"

"I don't want your goddamn money, Doc. I want what's mine."

What's his...

Oh, god.

Was this man some sort of sexual predator? Was he actually going to try to rape her right here, in the middle of a fucking field?

"Please," she begged him. "You don't want to—"

The man reached up and pulled the hood off. From their left, the moon shone brightly in the night sky.

Bright enough to show his face.

Sophie got a good, long look at the man hovering over her. Yet, she still couldn't believe her own eyes.

"Colton?" She gasped. "But I thought...the news said you were dead."

Jason said they had his *DNA*.

He held up his left hand, which was wrapped in a thick, white bandage. Something she hadn't noticed until now.

Even with the copious amount of gauze, it was clear to see he was missing a finger.

"Small price to pay for a life of freedom and riches, don't you think?"

"What the hell are you talking about?"

"Don't worry." He climbed off of her. "We'll have plenty of time to chat on the way."

"On the way to where?"

"To wherever the bag is you had with you in Djibouti. Now, get up."

He wasn't making any sense. For a second, Sophie wondered if he was high on some sort of recreational drug. A hallucinogen maybe?

But then a memory struck. She saw Colton rifling through her bag in the hospital the day of the uprising. He hadn't been looking for ibuprofen. He'd been hiding something in her bag.

And whatever it was, was still there.

"What did you do?"

"Enough chit chat." He waved the gun at her. "Let's go."

With no other choice, Sophie awkwardly got back up to her feet and started walking up the embankment.

As she got closer to the top, she spotted a large truck. The front end was crumpled some, but it was still running.

You can't get into that truck. If you do, you're dead.

She stopped walking.

"What the hell are you doing? Get your ass in the truck!"

"No." She turned to face him. "I'm not going anywhere with you."

"Oh, but I think you will."

He swung the gun around, pointing it toward the car. From this angle, if the man was any kind of shot, he'd be able to hit Jason through his shattered window.

"No, don't!" Sophie panicked.

"I don't want to kill your boyfriend, Doc. But I will, if I have to. Now tell me, where's the bag you had in Djibouti?"

"It's at the hospital," she spoke the truth. "It's been in my locker since I returned from Africa."

It was her go-bag. Her spare stethoscope, blood pressure cuff, and some basic first-aid supplies were still in there from the trip. Other than her time in Djibouti, she'd always kept it at work in case there was an incident requiring her to leave the hospital to treat a patient on-site.

Another thought hit her. This one nearly knocking her to the ground.

He's the one who broke into my house. Colton's the one who...

"It was you." Sophie stared back at him with utter shock. "You were in my house. You son of a bitch, you *shot* me."

A sudden rush of anger took over the fear. She not only welcomed it. She used it to keep herself in check.

"I didn't mean to shoot you!" Colton snapped back. "You were fighting for the gun and it went off. Trust me, Doc. If I wanted you dead, you'd be dead."

Keep him talking. If he's talking, he's not taking you away from Jason.

"I didn't notice your bandage then. But you must've been injured because the news said your body had been discovered a few days ago."

"I was wearing gloves," he ground out. "Now come on." He shoved the gun back in her direction. "Start walking or I swear to God, I'll shoot him."

Sophie looked back at the car. Through the window, she could see Jason in the same position he'd been in earlier.

He hadn't heard them. He was going to wake up, find her gone, and...he was going to blame himself.

Just like he still blames himself for what happened to Shelby.

Her heart shattered into a million pieces.

With no other choice—because she'd never risk Jason's life for her own—she looked back at the man she never really knew and nodded.

"Okay." A sad resolve rang through her terrified voice. "I'll go."

****

Jason woke with a start, Sophie's name flying from his lips as his eyes shot open.

"Sophie!" He tried sitting up, but someone was pushing against his chest.

From his right, a deep voice said, "Calm the hell down before you hurt yourself even worse."

Calm down? The fuck he would.

"Sophie!" He pushed against the man and—

"Goddamn it, Ryker, stop!"

Jason focused on the man's face, his vision slightly delayed as he tried to figure out who the guy was standing outside his shattered window.

"Jake?"

"There he is." Relief filled the other man's blue eyes. "You're hurt. You need to—"

"I need to find Sophie."

"And we will. But first, we need to make sure you aren't seriously injured."

We?

With another series of blinks, Jason realized Trevor was also there. Only he was *inside* the car with one hand on his wrist to check his pulse while the other pressed a pad of gauze to his throbbing forehead.

"He took her." He jerked his hand free from Trevor's grasp. "He fucking took her right out from under my goddamn nose!"

Ah, god. He couldn't lose her.

Not again. Not Sophie.

"We were hit, and I was knocked out cold. Ow!" He recoiled from where Trevor was treating his headwound. "Motherfucker, that hurts."

"Sorry, man. You've got a pretty big gash here. Probably gonna need stitches."

"I don't have time for fucking stitches. Just put some of that glue shit on there, slap a band aid over it, and get the hell out so I can go find Soph."

Trevor looked over Jason's head to Jake. Begrudgingly, Jake gave Trevor a nod, and the former Delta medic began doing as Jason had ordered.

"Wait," Jason thought of something. "How did you two even know to come here?"

"I called your phone," he quickly explained. "Liv knew Sophie was upset after hearing the news of Moore's death, and she wanted me to ask if we could stop by your place tomorrow so she could check on her. Sophie answered the call and told me about the wreck."

Jesus. He'd been out cold for that entire conversation.

"I jumped in the truck and told Sophie to hang up so I could call 911. Then I called Trev and told him to head this direction. Figured we could get to you guys before an ambulance would."

"We have to go." He tried opening his door, but it was jammed. To Trevor, he said, "You finished yet? I need you to move so I can get the hell out of here."

"Almost done. It'll go a hell of a lot faster if you'd quit moving your ass around."

Fuck!

It took everything he had, but Jason forced himself to sit still while Trevor finished dressing his wound.

"Tell me what you remember," Jake ordered calmly.

"Not a lot. I was out cold for...I don't know how long. Then I started going in and out of consciousness. I could hear Sophie talking to someone, but I couldn't wake up enough to move or holler out for her."

What a fucking nightmare that was. To know his woman was in danger...to be *this* close and not be able to do anything about it.

"I heard a man yelling at her. He had a gun, and..."

A flash of a memory struck. One so brief, Jason wasn't even sure it was real. Sophie screaming and then...

"She said his name." Jason stared back at Jake, fear and disbelief turning his veins to ice. "It was Colton. I heard her say the name Colton."

"As in Colton Moore?" Jake's brows rose high.

It was him. Jason knew in his swirling *gut* it was him.

The person who'd taken Sophie was a man everyone thought was dead.

"Ah Christ, I think I'm going to be sick."

Nausea churned in his stomach like a bubbling pot filled with acid.

"Swallow that shit down, Ryker," Trevor ordered harshly. "I'm not about to get puked on by your sorry ass."

Jason knew what the other man was doing. He was taking control and barking orders to snap him out of whatever mindfuck he had going on at the moment.

The dickhead's plan worked, too, because Jason was able to breathe through the sickening fear without actually getting sick.

Trevor gave him a nod. "There ya go."

"We good?"

"As good as we can be given the circumstances."

"Then get the fuck out of my way."

Jason knew he was being an asshole, but right now he couldn't care less.

Sophie was out there, somewhere. She *needed* him, and he was not going to let her down.

Ignoring the incessant dizziness threatening to consume him, Jason finally managed to climb his way out of the mangled car.

"We have to find her," he told both men as soon as he was outside and on his feet. They rushed up the embankment to where Jake and Trevor's trucks were parked. "Moore's going to...he's going to fucking *kill* her as soon as he gets what he wants."

The sound of her screaming as she was pulled from the car would haunt him the rest of his life.

"You don't know that." Jake was shaking his head before he'd even finished talking.

"Yes, I fucking *do* know that!" He shouted at his friend. "I can feel it in my gut."

And *Christ*, that feeling was tearing him up inside.

Sirens blared and red and blue lights filled the night sky as the ambulance and other emergency vehicles drove up on the scene.

Jake thought for a moment and then, "Fine." He focused on the paramedics rushing toward them with a gurney. "We'll go just as soon as the medic releases you."

"Fuck that." Jason started to shake his head, then thought better of it. "We'll go now."

"Your ass gets released, or I'm strapping you to that gurney and taking you to the hospital my damn self."

Jason looked at the two, uniformed women standing next to them, now. Then he looked back at Jake. "Do I have your word on that?"

"Of course."

"Good." He gave one of the medics a nod. "I want to sign out AMA."

With her eyes glued to the bandage and blood on his face, she said, "Sir, I don't think that's a—"

"Get me the papers." He stared her down. "Now."

"Damn it, Jason," Jake hissed. "That is *not* what I meant, and you know it."

In a smart move, the paramedic grabbed a clipboard from the back of the ambulance and handed him that and a pen. Pointing to where he needed to sign, Jason scribbled his signature and handed it back to her.

Ignoring Jake's protests, he asked the woman, "Am I released?"

"Yes, sir. But I still think you should—"

"Let's go." He started for Jake's truck.

"Jesus Christ." Jake caught up to him. "Will you sit down before you fall on your ass?"

"Works for me. I can sit in your truck while you drive."

"Fuck me." Jake shook his head and growled. "The cops are going to want to take your statement."

"I'll give it to them later. After we find Sophie."

"You don't even know where to start looking."

His hand slid to his pocket, thinking he could call his team in on this, as well. But then remembered Jake telling him Sophie had used his phone. "Shit." He stopped cold. "My phone."

"What about it?"

"I need to bring my team in on this."

Because this was Sophie. For her, he needed *all* hands on deck.

"I've got it." Trevor raced back down the hill to the car. A few agonizing seconds later, he was jogging toward them, shaking his head. "It's not there."

"The fuck you mean, it's not there? It has to be."

Jake hollered for the others on the scene to get quiet. Jason watched as the other man pulled his own phone out. He tapped Jason's number then put it on speaker.

The men waited and listened. Through Jake's speaker they could hear Jason's phone ringing. But that was the only thing they heard.

"It's not here." He shot Jake a look. "Sophie must've taken it with her."

"Smart." Trevor put a hand on Jason's shoulder. "Now we can track her location."

For the first time since he'd regained consciousness, Jason was filled with hope.

Hope that she *still* had the phone, and that she wasn't far away

And hope that he could reach the woman he loved in time to save her.

Chapter 12

Sophie's heart felt like it was going to leap out of her chest as she and Colton approached the staff locker room inside Homeland's private hospital.

Since she was an employee, they were able to enter through the secured parking garage, rather than deal with the security guard and his wand at the front doors.

On the way there, Colton had made her drive while he laid down in the back seat. She assumed this was because the world was supposed to think he was dead. If someone spotted him, it would put a huge ass wrench into his plan.

His crazy, fucked-up plan.

The man had rambled on during the drive into the city. He'd told her how he'd overheard Qasim talking with a man named Asad Al-Karim. Apparently, they'd been on the phone in some abandoned building Colton had been photographing, and Qasim had the phone on speaker.

Colton told her all about it. How Karim—the president of Syria—had orchestrated the riots and violence that had ensued on Djibouti when she'd been there. He'd also said Karim was behind several other violent attacks in the surrounding countries, and that the psychopathic leader was well on his way to making them all under his ruling.

Because he spoke fluent Arabic, Colton had understood everything Qasim and Karim were saying. Seeing it as an opportunity, he began recording the scene with his camera.

The idiot actually thought he could use the footage to blackmail Karim. But the plan backfired when the Syrian leader decided to send his people in after him.

Karim ordered his men to find Colton, and somehow Colton caught on. So, he disappeared and then faked his own death by killing some innocent drifter and then burning the body so it would be unrecognizable.

The crazed man cut off his own finger so they'd think it was him!

"I don't understand." Sophie spoke quietly as they walked down the hall. "You know Karim isn't going to pay you for the footage, so why do you want it so badly?"

The footage that, according to Colton, was on a jump drive he'd hidden in her bag.

"Do you have any idea how much a video like that is worth?" He snorted, pulling the ballcap he was now donning to keep his face hidden from the building's security cameras. "The mainstream media will be salivating over this shit. They'll pay *millions* for the exclusive rights, not only to the video, but also the interview I'll give after the footage is released. Of course, I'll be far away in some undisclosed location. Someplace that doesn't have extradition. Because I'm sure your boyfriend and his buddies who saved you will want to find me and teach me a lesson."

He laughed—actually laughed.

Her heart physically hurt as she thought about Jason lying hurt and alone in that car. Tears pricked the corners of her eyes as she silently prayed Jake had found him by now.

She kept telling herself that he had, and that Jason was going to be okay.

He had to be. For her, there was no other option.

They approached the door to the locker room. The man beside her was certifiable if he thought he was going to get away with what he'd done, but she had no choice but to do as he said.

He's gotten away with everything so far.

Sophie hesitated, but then opened the door. Her only saving grace was that if Colton really was planning to do what he said, there'd be no reason to kill her. All she had to do was give him the jump drive and let him walk away.

He was right about one thing...Jason would hunt him down. Jason, R.I.S.C., they'd all want justice for what this greedy bastard had done.

"Hey, Dr. Ruiz." One of the nightshift nurses came around the corner. "I didn't think you were working tonight."

The throbbing in her arm had gotten worse, and it was all she could do not to throw up on the floor. But she pushed it back and forced a steady voice.

"I'm not." Sophie smiled at the other woman. "I just needed to get something out of my locker."

Please leave. Please, please leave.

"Ugh, I hate it when I do that." The nurse laughed. "Okay, well I'd better get back out there. Have a good night!"

The second she left, Sophie went to the door and flipped the deadbolt to keep anyone else from coming in. The last thing she needed was for an innocent staff member to get caught up in her nightmare.

"Good girl. Now get the damn bag, and I'll be out of your hair for good."

Wanting nothing more, Sophie rushed to her locker. She fumbled with the padlock a couple of times, her nerves and broken wrist making it more than a little difficult to get the combination just right.

When she finally got the lock free, she opened the metal door and pulled her bag off the hook.

"I'll take that." He grabbed it out of her hand.

"There. You have what you want. Just...go."

"Thanks for your help, Doc. It's been a pleasure."

Sophie held her breath and waited. Colton turned to leave, but right as he took a step toward the door, the deadbolt turned, and another employee walked inside.

It was Daryl, one of the night security guards. He must have been out making his rounds. And since he was security, he had a key to the room.

At first, he looked confused, but then he recognized Colton's face. A second later, all hell broke loose.

"You're that journalist. The one from the news."

Moving lightning fast, Colton pulled his gun and wrapped an arm around Sophie's neck. Using her body as a shield, he pressed the gun's barrel against her temple.

"Remove your gun and toss it over to me."

"Whoa!" Daryl held his hands up. "What the hell, man?"

"Just do it!"

"Okay, okay." The kind man did as he was told. He pulled his weapon from his holster, acted as though he were going to throw it over to them. Instead, he decided to be a hero and raised the weapon in Colton's direction.

In a panic, Colton fired his gun, hitting Daryl in the middle of his forehead. The poor man was dead before he ever hit the ground.

"Fuck!"

Sophie's scream got caught in her throat. So much violence. God, she was sick of the *violence.*

"You need to run," she told the man holding her hostage.

"I can't fucking run, now!" He yelled. "The cops will be swarming this place before I get the chance to leave!"

"That's not true," Sophie lied. "There's no way someone didn't hear that shot, so yeah. The cops will be headed this way. But you still have time. If you go right now, you can go out the way we came in. You'll be gone before the police get here."

He was considering it. She could practically feel his wheels turning.

Colton started to loosen his hold, but at the last second he held her tight and said, "Fine. I'll go. But you're coming with me."

"What? No!" Sophie shook her head wildly. "You can move faster without me."

"But if they do show up, I'll need insurance. Something to keep them from shooting my ass. Come on." He began walking them to the door. "You're exactly what I need to get myself out of this mess."

Walking awkwardly together, they made their way across the room and to the door. Sophie forced herself not to look at Daryl's lifeless body, for fear she'd break down completely and get herself killed.

Oh, god.

She thought about Jason. Wondered how he was. Where he was.

And as they entered the hallway, Sophie wondered if she'd ever see him again.

****

Jason ran to the nurse working the front desk. "Have you seen Dr. Ruiz?"

Alarmed by his sudden appearance and excited tone, she shook her head. "No. Dr. Ruiz isn't on the schedule for tonight."

"I know she's not on the schedule. I'm asking if you've seen her."

"What about this man?" Jake held up a picture of Colton Moore.

"The dead guy? Uh, no." She chuckled. "Haven't seen him, either, except for on the news. Did something happen? Is Dr. Ruiz in some sort of trouble?"

Ignoring her, Jason, Jake, and Trevor proceeded to ask the same questions to every employee they saw. They all had the same answer.

No one had seen Sophie or Moore.

"Fuck!" Jason's loud voice boomed.

"Easy, Ryker. Your phone's still pinged to this location. They have to be here."

"Just because my phone's here, doesn't mean Sophie's still here."

Or that she's still alive.

"She's here," Trevor assured him. "We just have to keep looking."

Jason felt as though he was losing his damn mind. He couldn't lose her. Not now. Not when they'd just—

"Did you say you're looking for Dr.Ruiz?" A soft voice reached their ears from behind.

All three men spun around to see a middle-aged nurse facing them.

"Yes!" Jason blurted. "Have you seen her?"

"Yeah."

He began a succession of rapid-fire questions.

"When?"

"Just a couple of minutes ago. Why, is something—"

"Where did you see her?

"S-she was in the employee locker room."

"Was she alone?"

"No. There was a man with her."

"Is this him?" Jake showed her the same picture of Moore.

"Yeah. I mean, he had a hat on, but I'm pretty sure that was him."

"Let's go!"

Jason took off in a dead sprint down the hallway toward the locker room. Because this hospital was his creation, he knew exactly where the room was located.

Hold on, baby. I'm coming.

With Jake and Trevor in tow, they were halfway to the place Sophia was last seen when a gunshot blasted, the echoing sound stopping Jason's entire world.

No!

"Sophie!" Pushing his legs to their limits, Jason pulled his gun from his holster as he ran.

He was less than two yards away when he saw her.

Sophie had just exited the locker room. The fact that she was alive and appeared to be okay registered a second before he saw the gun.

Moore, the fucker, had her in a choke hold. His gun was pressed against her skull, and his finger was dangerously close to the trigger.

"Don't come any closer, or I'll shoot!" Moore warned.

Jason and the others froze in their tracks.

"Let her go!" he yelled.

A few screams and hurried footfalls came from somewhere nearby. But Jason didn't take his focus off the man in his sights.

"I let her go, I'm dead!" Colton hollered back.

"You don't let her go, you'll be dead," Jason vowed. "You don't want to do this, Colton. I know you don't want to hurt Sophie."

He knew no such thing, but he had to play the game.

"I don't. I didn't want to hurt anyone. I just wanted—"

"It doesn't matter," Jake chimed in, his weapon trained on Moore. "Whatever you wanted, whatever your plans were, it's over. The only way out is to let Sophie go."

Jason thought he was going to do it. He thought Moore was going to let her go and turn himself over.

He should've known better. He should've anticipated the man's next move.

He didn't.

Everything all happened at once. Several horrifying actions occurring simultaneously.

Moore shoved Sophie forward. She stumbled and nearly fell. Jason ran to her as Moore raised his gun and pointed it in her direction.

He's going to shoot her!

The past morphed with the present. Another woman's face. Another time. Another shooter.

Not this time! Not my Sophie!

"Get down!" Jason yelled. He shoved Sophie out of the way.

Gunfire blasted through the hall, several bullets flying through the air at once.

Jason saw Moore fly backward as he, Jake, and Trevor filled him with holes. Moore hit the cold, hard tile. His lifeless body bouncing as it landed.

For several seconds no one moved. Jason wasn't sure he was even breathing. And then...

"Jason!" Sophie was on her feet and throwing herself into his arms.

With his gun still in his hand, he wrapped his arms around the woman he loved and held on for dear life.

"Baby!" He closed his eyes and drew in her sweet scent. "Thank God you're okay."

When Jason held her a little tighter, Sophie released a small cry. He recognized the sound as one of pain rather than fear.

"Soph?" He pulled back just enough to see her face, unsure of what he'd done to hurt her. "What is it, baby?"

Holding her right arm snuggly against her, Sophie slid a glance to the man lying in a pool of his own blood. "It's my arm. It broke when he hit us, and the car rolled into that field."

A murderous rage toward a dead man engulfed him. Jason felt the angry burn deep inside his chest

The fire grew. He brought a hand to his chest, rubbing against the source in order to ease the discomfort there.

Sophie was okay. He had to remind himself of that. Her arm was hurt, but she was still here despite Moore's efforts to take her away from him.

Jason rubbed his chest harder because... *Christ, that hurts.*

The pain was almost unbearable, now. He pulled his hand back and glanced down, confused when he saw blood.

What the...

His knees started to give out.

"Jason!" Sophie reached for him with her good arm. "Oh, my god! He's been shot!"

I have?

He looked down at his chest. The crimson stain spreading across his stark white shirt undeniable.

Well, hell.

"I need help!" Sophie screamed down the hall to someone he couldn't see.

The panic in her voice registered as Jake and Trevor grabbed onto him to keep him from falling. They carefully laid him down onto the floor.

"Gunshot wound to the right upper chest!" Jason felt Sophie's hand rubbing along his back. "Anterior entry, no exit wound!"

Shit. That meant the bullet was still in him.

"I'm...okay," he lied.

"Shh...don't talk." Sophie yanked his shirt open, buttons flying as she began assessing his wound.

Several staff members rushed over to them. In seconds, he was moved to a gurney and rushed down the hall. Sophie spouted off all sorts of medical shit he didn't understand, but that was okay.

He was content just watching her.

She's incredible.

Sophie was in doctor-mode, now. Seeing her in action had always amazed him. Seeing it from *this* perspective gave him a whole new appreciation for what she did.

"Soph..." He reached for her, his arm struggling to follow his mental command.

Why does it feel so heavy?

"I'm here." She grabbed his hand with her uninjured one. "I'm right here, and you're going to be just fine."

It was the first time she'd ever lied to him.

Jason felt himself fading. His vision began closing in all around him, and...he knew he was dying.

But before he did, before he left this world and the woman walking beside him behind, he had to tell her...

"L-love...you." She needed to know that.

Silver streaks traveled down Sophie's cheeks as she stared at him and said, "I love you, too. So much."

Jason smiled. At least, he thought he was smiling.

She loves me.

Jason wanted to tell her not to cry. He wanted to remind her how strong and fierce she was. That she was the most amazing woman he'd ever known.

It broke his heart to know she'd feel the same sort of pain he had when he lost Shelby all those years ago. But if anyone could survive everything she had, it was her.

I should tell her that. She needs to know everything was going to be okay.

He tried to do just that. But his eyes had already closed, and the woman he loved more than anything in this world had faded away.

Chapter 13

Sophie sat by Jason's bedside. Resting her new, blue cast on the mattress beside him, she kept his limp hand in hers while she watched his chest rise up and down with slow, even breaths.

It was a miracle he was still alive.

The bullet had entered his chest below his right collarbone, nicking his lung causing a pneumothorax. The surgeon—a world-renowned doctor she trusted implicitly—had made sure she was kept abreast of his progress during the four-hour procedure.

Jake and Trevor had stayed with her the entire time. Olivia and sweet little Lily joining them the minute they heard the news.

The rest of R.I.S.C. and their spouses—both Alpha *and* Bravo Teams—had also showed soon after the shooting. So had Jason's own team within his covert Homeland unit.

It had brought Sophie comfort seeing the private waiting room bursting at the seams with men and women who loved Jason as much as she did.

And she *did* love him.

As unexplainable as it seemed, what she felt for the man lying pale and weak before her was as real as anything she'd ever experienced before.

I almost lost him.

Tears streamed down her face, as she replayed the moment the surgeon's nurse had come to tell her Jason had crashed on the operating table.

Twice.

His beautiful, selfless, loving heart had stopped beating. It *stopped*. That thought alone was enough to nearly break her.

But as Sophie brushed her thumb across the back of his hand, the machines tracking each of his precious heartbeats reminded her that he hadn't given up.

He'd fought to come back. To her. To his friends. *That's* what she had to hold on to.

As the hours passed, she thought of their whirlwind romance, and all they'd shared and experienced in an insanely short amount of time.

Every so often, flashes of other memories—unpleasant memories—would force their way inside.

The gunshots. Seeing the blood on Jason's white shirt. The horrifying realization that he'd been shot.

Emotions threatened to overpower her, but Sophie held back. She needed to stay strong and focus on the positive...

I didn't lose him.

As she sat by his side, Sophie watched as Jason's lungs did their job by pulling in precious oxygen. She relished in the fact that his strong heart was still giving him life by pumping blood through his arteries and veins.

Love...you.

The words he'd spoken to her right before losing consciousness were the most sacred words she'd ever heard.

He loved her, and she loved him. He'd fought to live, and right there in that quiet hospital room, Sophie vowed to give him the life he'd always wanted.

Leaning up over the railing, she pressed her lips to his forehead, letting them linger.

"Come back to me soon, honey," she whispered. "I'll be here, waiting. For as long as it takes."

****

Jason woke to the sound of low murmurs. He was pretty sure Jake was there, along with his wife and daughter. But there was another voice reaching his ears. The only voice he truly longed to hear.

Sophie.

"I'm right here."

She'd heard that? Jason was confused at first, but then realized he must've said her name out loud.

Peeling his eyes open, he blinked against the fog to find her. "Soph?"

Damn, his voice sounded rough, even to him.

"I'm right here," she repeated.

And she was.

"Hey." She gave him a wide, watery smile.

"Hi."

Jason watched as a flood of tears fell from her eyes.

The last time he saw her cry was when she thought he was dying. For a moment there, he was sure he would.

It would've been so easy. To just give up and let himself slip away.

A year ago—hell a *month* ago—he probably would have given into the peaceful abyss that had been calling his name while the doctors worked to save him. But now...

I have too much to live for.

"About time your lazy ass woke up." A smiling Jake entered his vision next to Sophie.

"Fuck...off." Jason told his friend playfully.

Christ, he felt weak.

Olivia, Jake, and Sophie all laughed. Even little Lily let out a squeal of delight.

Not caring they had an audience, Sophie planted a kiss on Jason's desert-dry lips. "Now I know for sure you're going to be okay."

"Couldn't leave...you," he rasped.

"Good." She pressed a hand to his face. "What do you say we don't do that again, yeah?"

"I'll always...protect...you." It was the God's honest truth.

Her eyes softened as they began to well again. "I love you. I said that before, but I wasn't sure if you heard me."

"I heard you." His voice got a bit stronger. "And I love you, too."

Smiling wide, Sophie pressed her lips to his mouth. His chin. The tip of his nose.

Jake cleared his throat. "We'll take that as our cue to leave."

"Good idea," Jason teased the other man.

More chuckles ensued as Jake and Olivia said their goodbyes before leaving him alone with Sophie.

As soon as they were gone, Sophie asked him, "How do you feel?"

"Like I've been shot in the chest."

With a sideways grin, she held up a small device attached to a cord. "This is a morphine drip. It's connected to your IV. If you start hurting too much and I'm not here, press this button and you'll be administered more pain meds. And before you think about going crazy with the stuff, the doses are controlled."

Sophie's beautiful brown eyes lit up with humor, but he also saw a storm of emotions building.

"Don't need drugs." He stared back at her. "I just need you."

When he reached for her hand, his fingers brushed something hard and rough. Glancing down, he noticed the fresh cast that had been formed around her right arm from her elbow down.

"Damn. I forgot about your arm. Are you okay? Does it hurt?"

"It's a bit achy." She shrugged. "Nothing like a bullet to the chest."

He could tell her words were meant as a joke, but Sophie's voice cracked at the very end. Right before she completely broke down.

A new pain hit his chest, and it had nothing to do with his wound.

"Come here." Ignoring the pull of the stitches that had been put in hours before, he scooted over as far as he could and coaxed her onto the bed with him.

"I don't want to...hurt...you," she protested between stuttering breaths, even as she snuggled up beside him.

"The only thing hurting me is seeing you upset." Jason smoothed the hair on the back of her head. "I'm going to be okay. We both are."

"I was...so...scared." Sophie continued to cry.

She's breaking my heart.

"So was I," Jason admitted in the privacy of his room.

"You?" She looked up at him. "I didn't think anything scared you."

"There's one thing." He swallowed a huge knot that had suddenly formed in his throat. "One thing that absolutely terrifies me."

"What's that?"

"Losing you."

"Jason." More tears formed. "You won't."

"I want a life with you, Sophie," he stated boldly. "All that stuff we talked about before? I want that, but only if I can have it with you."

"I want that, too." She wiped her cheeks dry. "It's all I've ever wanted."

"Good. Now that we got that settled, what do you say we fly to Vegas as soon as I'm sprung from this place?"

"Vegas?" Her dark brows pulled together. "You want us to take a vacation?"

"I want us to get married."

It took a full two seconds for his words to sink in. "What?"

"I know it's fast, but we also know what we want and who we want it with. Why waste more time when you and I both know where this is headed?"

A slow smile spread across her gorgeous face. "I like your logic, Agent Ryker."

"Is that a yes?"

"Yes." Sophie nodded, her cheeks becoming damp once more. "Yes, I'll marry you."

Pain forgotten, Jason guided her lips to his. "I like your answer, Dr. Ruiz."

"Good." She kissed him again. "Although, what would you think if I changed my title to Dr. Ryker?"

Jason's heart swelled, the machines around them beeping a bit faster. "I think that sounds fucking perfect."

Epilogue

Six weeks later...

"Here ya go." Jake handed Jason another beer.

"Thanks, man." Jason took the bottle and smirked. "You know, I could get used to everyone waiting on me like this."

"Well, don't." The other man sat down in the empty lawn chair beside him. "Only reason I'm doing it now is because my wife said I should bring that to you."

Jason shot Jake a raised brow. "And you always do everything Olivia says?"

"Pretty much." Jake shrugged. "You're next, you know. Better get used to it."

Jason knew his friend was full of shit. He lived to make his wife happy. And Olivia did the same for him.

Theirs was the kind of marriage he wanted with Sophie. The kind he knew they were going to have.

After being released from the hospital, they'd decided to put her house on the market, and she'd moved in with him. It took all of two weeks to receive an offer she was happy with, and they'd closed the deal another week after that.

Jason would've been fine selling his place and moving into hers, but Sophie hadn't wanted that. She'd told him she'd fallen in love with his place on sight. That it was perfect.

Just like her.

Prior to his release, Jason had worked from his hospital bed to close the investigation into Colton Moore. He still couldn't believe the dumbass had thought his plan was a good one.

Men like Asad Al-Karim did not take kindly to things such as blackmail. It was a lesson Moore had learned the hard way...with his life.

The one good thing that had come from it all—aside from him and Sophie's relationship—was that Asad had been arrested for his terroristic crimes.

The former Syrian president was currently being held in a classified location within the United States. His younger brother, Sarim Al-Karim, had since taken his place as President.

From all accounts, Sarim was the 'good' brother, and had nothing but good intentions for his country. Jason and his team had been watching him closely, and from what he'd seen so far, Sarim had already begun to rebuild trust with the Syrian people.

"You think things will truly calm down for Syria now that Asad is out of the picture?" Jake seemed to read his mind.

"Sure as hell hope so." Jason took a slow pull from his beer. "I'm surprised Sarim stepped in after what his brother did, but all of our intel points to him being one of the good guys."

"What's going to happen to Asad?"

"You know how that shit works. They'll get what they can from him, and then…"

Jason didn't finish his sentence. He didn't have to.

Men like Asad had a way of disappearing. And the world will be a much better place when that finally happens.

Sophie strolled across Jake and Olivia's back patio and sat down on Jason's lap.

His fiancée was a vision in her long, flowered sundress and sandals. Her hair flowing freely around her shoulders and down her back.

God, I can't wait to marry her.

He'd been serious about the Vegas wedding, but they'd decided to hold off until he was completely cleared from the doctor. Neither one wanted anything to get in the way of their special day…or the honeymoon.

"Hey, you." Jason took the kiss she'd offered.

"Hey, yourself. You got a second to talk?"

"I'll go help with the food." Jake rose to his feet and gave them a tip of his bottle before leaving in search of his wife.

"You were right." Jason pulled Sophie in a little closer.

"I usually am," she teased. "But what exactly was I right about this time?"

"Accepting Jake and Liv's invitation for dinner. I'm glad we came."

He was still getting used to having a more social relationship with Jake and his teams. He'd always felt awkward being around all the happy couples, but now...

I'm half of my very own happy couple.

"You said we needed to talk?" He brought his focus back to the present. "You haven't changed your mind about marrying me, have you?"

Sophie laughed. "Not a chance. But there is something I need to tell you. Something I found out when I went to the doctor today to get my cast removed."

His stomach clenched and his chest tightened. "Is something wrong? Damn it, I knew I should've gone with you."

"I'm fine." She put a hand to his worried face. "But while I was there, my doctor noticed it had been a while since I'd had some routine blood-work done."

"Okay..."

The hesitation—and nervousness—in her eyes ramped his anxiety to an uncomfortable level.

"Baby, you're scaring me," he confessed. "Just tell me."

Sophie's delicate throat worked as she swallowed. "They found something...unexpected."

"Unexpected as in..."

She released a slow breath and locked her gaze with his. "As in...I'm pregnant."

He heard the words. He even knew what they meant. But it still took Jason's shocked brain a moment to actually process them.

"You're...pregnant?"

She nodded. "Six weeks."

Six weeks. That meant she'd conceived around the time they'd first slept together.

The memory of Moore pointing his gun toward her that day in the hospital flashed through his mind.

Holy shit. I could've lost her. I could've lost them both.

But he hadn't this time. Sophie was fine, and she was....

"You're pregnant," he whispered in awe.

"I am." Sophie nodded. "We are."

"We're going to have a baby." A slow smile grew on his face, not stopping until it was stretched from ear to ear. "We're going to have a baby!"

He shot up from the chair with Sophie cradled in his arms. Spinning them around, he shouted the words again. This time, saying them loud enough for Jake and Olivia—and probably anyone within a ten-mile radius—to hear.

"We're going to have a baby!"

Hearing the news, Olivia and Jake came rushing over to them. The expression on their faces a mixture of shock and joy.

Before they joined them, Jason took advantage of their remaining seconds alone to slam his mouth to Sophie's. He kissed her with all the love and joy filling his heart, and prayed she knew just how happy she'd made him.

He was going to be a dad. He was going to be a husband.

And thanks to the woman wrapped in his loving, protective arms, Jason knew he was the luckiest man in the world.

Pre-order the R.I.S.C. Series Finale

His Greatest Risk (R.I.S.C. 10)[1]
Don't miss out on this exciting series finale...Coming June 2021
A man searching for a purpose. A woman searching for love. A monster out to destroy R.I.S.C...and anyone who gets in his way.

Former Delta Force operator Trace Winters is an expert at two things: Finding the bad guys and taking them down. The instinct he was born with and the skills he's learned make him the perfect candidate to lead R.I.S.C.'s new Charlie Team. But when Trace accepts a job working for Jake McQueen—his former SF teammate and friend—he quickly realizes he's gotten more than he ever bargained for.

Emma Cooper has always lived life to its fullest. From skydiving to culinary classes, there isn't much she hasn't done...except fall in love. While working a temp job at R.I.S.C., she meets Trace—a sexy, breath-stealing man who makes her knees weak and her insides quiver. But just when Emma decides to make her attraction for the hunky security expert known, all hell breaks loose and R.I.S.C. falls under attack.

With an unknown force out for revenge and his new boss critically injured, Trace steps in to help Alpha Team win their toughest battle yet. But when Emma becomes the madman's next target, Trace will risk everything to keep the woman he's falling for safe.

Pre-Order Now:
His Greatest Risk (R.I.S.C. 10)[2]

---

1. https://a.nzn.to/2Rg9rzH
2. https://a.nzn.to/2Rg9rzH

Want to read more from Ms. Blakely's R.I.S.C. Series?

See how it all started with Jake and the rest of Alpha Team by checking out the other books in this series:

Book 1: Taking a Risk, Part One[1] (Jake & Olivia's HFN)
Book 2: Taking a Risk, Part Two[2] (Jake & Olivia's HEA)
Book 3: Beautiful Risk[3] (Trevor & Lexi)
Book 4: Intentional Risk[4] (Derek & Charlie)
Book 5: Unpredictable Risk[5] (Grant & Brynnon)
Book 6: Ultimate Risk[6] (Coop & Mac)
Book 7: Targeted Risk[7] (Mike & Jules)
Book 9: Undeniable Risk[8] (Ryker & Sophie)
Book 10: His Greatest Risk[9] (Series Finale)

---

1. https://www.amazon.com/TAKING-RISK-PART-R-I-S-C-Book-ebook/dp/B07KV1WN2M/ref=sr_1_1?ie=UTF8&qid=1545935537&sr=8-1&keywords=taking+a+risk+part+one

2. http://bit.ly/TakingaRiskPartTwoAmzn

3. http://bit.ly/Beautiful_Risk

4. https://www.amazon.com/s?k=intentional+risk&ref=nb_sb_noss

5. https://www.amazon.com/Unpredictable-Risk-R-I-S-C-Book-5-ebook/dp/B08121Q22T/ref=sr_1_1?keywords=unpredictable+risk&qid=1583071266&sr=8-1

6. https://www.amazon.com/Ultimate-Risk-R-I-S-C-Book-6-ebook/dp/B083BGX9VR/ref=pd_sim_351_1/136-7699527-9116030?_encoding=UTF8&pd_rd_i=B083BGX9VR&pd_rd_r=c6105876-607b-4f69-bd90-b969a3900acb&pd_rd_w=GnGzP&pd_rd_wg=VpL69&pf_rd_p=65e3eab0-d81f-4a76-93ff-f0b7b1d6cd3d&pf_rd_r=CT47DHN02D3Q25JEF1DZ&psc=1&refRID=CT47DHN02D3Q25JEF1DZ

7. https://www.amazon.com/dp/B088SND1VZ/ref=sr_1_2?dchild=1&keywords=targeted+risk&qid=1589837961&sr=8-2

8. https://www.amazon.com/Undeniable-Risk-R-I-S-C-Book-9-ebook/dp/B08NGYKKX8/ref=sr_1_1?dchild=1&keywords=undeniable+risk&qid=1616870521&sr=8-1

9. https://amzn.to/2Rg9rzH

Check out R.I.S.C.'s Bravo Team!

Click below to read Ms. Blakely's R.I.S.C. spin-off series in Susan Stoker's Special Forces: Operation Alpha World:
Book 1: Rescuing Gracelynn[1] (Nate & Gracie)
Book 2: Rescuing Katherine[2] (Matt & Katherine)
Book 3: Rescuing Gabriella[3] (Zade & Gabby)
Book 4: Rescuing Ellena[4] (Gabe & Elle)
Book 5: Rescuing Jenna[5] (Adrian & Jenna)

---

1. https://amzn.to/2KOap0o
2. https://www.amazon.com/Rescuing-Katherine-Special-Forces-Operation-ebook/dp/B085GH6HQQ/ref=sr_1_1?dchild=1&keywords=rescuing+katherine&qid=1589836951&sr=8-1
3. https://www.amazon.com/gp/product/B08C45WWYQ?pf_rd_r=TQEKRB704P6TQ6GK3YCB&pf_rd_p=edaba0ee-c2fe-4124-9f5d-b31d6b1bfbee
4. https://www.amazon.com/Rescuing-Ellena-Special-Forces-Operation-ebook/dp/B08M3RD-DZ2/ref=sr_1_1?dchild=1&keywords=rescuing+ellena&qid=1615829805&sr=8-1
5. https://amzn.to/3qMxbHS

Rescuing Gracelynn Blurb

(Book 1 in Ms. Blakely's R.I.S.C. spin-off series, Bravo Team)
"Anna Blakely has another hit book! This exciting story is filled with action, drama, excitement, romance, terror and much, much more. If you want a book that pulls you in and keeps you excited to turn the next page, over and over again, then I highly recommend reading RESCUING GRACELYNN!"
- Bookbub reviewer

He Never Believed In True Love...Until He Met Her.
Bravo Team's technical analyst and confirmed bachelor, Nathan Carter, is happy being single and has no intention of falling under the spell of a woman. Ever. Then, he meets Gracelynn. Before he knows it, the sweet, tenacious woman has Nate questioning his long-standing doubts about love, soul mates, and happily ever after.

Gracie McDaniels is happy with her new life and loves her new job. Working closely with the hunky guys on R.I.S.C.'s Bravo Team, including her future brother-in-law's best friend, doesn't seem as if it'll be an issue. Then, she meets him.

Nate's smart, funny, and handsome...everything she's ever wanted in a partner. But just as they start to grow close, an innocent friendship from Gracie's past comes back to haunt her. When her life is threatened, Gracie instinctively turns to Nate for protection and soon he and the other members of Bravo step up to keep Gracie safe.

With help from Ghost and his friends, the Delta Force and Bravo teams find themselves racing against the clock to save the only woman Nate has ever loved...before it's too late.

Excerpt from Rescuing Gracelynn

"Are you okay?" Her question came out much softer than she'd meant for it to.

Nate gave her a humorless smirk as he shoved his hands into his pockets. "I should be asking you that question."

"I'm...better." And she was. The pounding in her head had quieted to a dull ache, and the intense trembling had subsided.

When he continued to just stand there, staring without saying another word, Gracie realized he was probably waiting for an apology. One that was well-deserved.

Standing, she laid what was left of the ice pack down onto her seat's cushion and began to say what needed to be said. "I'm really sorry, Nate. We never should have left the building without one of you. Or, at the very least, we should have checked with you beforehand."

She waited, but he remained silent. *Okay.* Apparently, more groveling was going to be involved.

Stepping toward him, Gracie nervously continued. "I-I know it wasn't very smart of us, and you and Kole have every right to be upset. It's just that, I was exhausted from going over everything with Jake and the others, and then doing the sketch with Dalton. Sarah mentioned coffee and I..."

She let her voice trail off, hoping he'd say *something*. Instead, he simply began walking slowly toward her, a muscle in his strong, sexy jaw bulging as he moved. The look he gave her was so intense, Gracie half-expected to see steam to start shooting out of his ears.

"Okay, look," she said defensively. "I get that you're upset, but we just wanted to go grab a quick coffee. That was it. I mean, you saw us, right? We were coming straight back. Yes, it was stupid, but you can't seriously stay mad about this forev—"

The rest of the word were cut off when he grabbed both her upper arms and slammed his mouth down onto hers.

A tiny squeak escaped the back of her throat just before he used his tongue to pry her lips apart. Apology forgotten, Gracie opened her mouth and let him in.

Standing in the middle of their boss's office, she held on tight as Nate began to devour her. He took and she gave. It was the most sensual, raw-emotions moment of her entire life.

When he was done feasting, Nate pulled away slowly and rested his forehead against hers. They remained locked in each other's arms, their chests moving in sync as they both attempted to catch their breath.

Regaining some control, Nate lifted his head and locked his eyes with hers. "I thought I'd lost you."

He sounded different than before. His voice was low and there was this dark edge to it she'd never heard before. "Nate?"

"You scared the shit out of me, baby." He swallowed hard and shook his head back and forth slowly. "Don't ever do that, again."

Click below to purchase your copy of Rescuing Gracelynn today!
https://amzn.to/2KOap0o[1]

---

1. https://amzn.to/2KOap0o?fbclid=IwAR2XwuNhIkTFWLuDgzaEiqKcBn3ixh-CILtWMJOuCfmFTbhq7bmGafgo2sWo

Want to connect with Anna?

Stalk her here...

- Newsletter signup (with FREE book!) BookHip.com/ZLMKFT[1]
  - Join Anna's Reader Group: www.facebook.com/groups/blakelysbunch/[2]
- BookBub: https://www.bookbub.com/authors/anna-blakely
  - Amazon: amazon.com/author/annablakely[3]
  - Author Page: https://www.facebook.com/annablakelyromance[4]
  - Instagram: https://instagram.com/annablakely
  - Twitter: @ablakelyauthor[5]
- Goodreads: https://www.goodreads.com/author/show/18650841.Anna_Blakely

---

1. http://bookhip.com/ZLMKFT?fbclid=IwAR2lZIGJqF5YrRpJSmgph5FGCa9xzhhHoTNFa4yvvQFKPmXMKh2xSoktIpM
2. http://www.facebook.com/groups/blakelysbunch/
3. http://amazon.com/author/annablakely
4. http://www.facebook.com/annablakelyromance
5. https://l.facebook.com/l.php?u=https%3A%2F%2Ftwitter.com%2Fablakelyauthor%3Ffbclid%3DIwAR3eBPASIFhD7fc5Uvma8eF1AjPCwmetlIl-zEAG669Eg_0amjNhVjuehBA&h=AT19i6MitKZ_vIjaH9n6aV1uqVHausvBKfm12jM2r_D1LlIg3g72VbbEiwpffDP3nXHZObcwB4I4xn2YaV_UCl10jr4V6lS4u5wy1bo0ka8ta8x0lEVP5f0A5fYaKa3crtTJLg